GIOVANNI

A DARK MAFIA ROMANCE

NATASHA KNIGHT

Copyright © 2018 by Natasha Knight

All rights reserved.

No part of this book may be reproduced in any form or by any electronic or mechanical means, including information storage and retrieval systems, without written permission from the author, except for the use of brief quotations in a book review.

For Diane D. and Kcee B.

I want you both to know how much I appreciate your constant friendship and support. It can be a pretty lonely business being a writer and I am so grateful that you are in my life both personally and professionally.

Thank you.

PROLOGUE
EMILIA

I can sleep. It's strange, but I can always sleep. I learned it on that grimy basement floor four years ago.

Sleep.

Forget.

Sleep until they wake you. Sleep until they make you.

The past has a way of creeping up on you.

Of repeating.

Reappearing.

I don't know if mine will ever be finished with me. I thought it would. I thought it had. I thought the night I crawled out of that window and away from that house, that I had beat it. That I had somehow survived.

But the thing with surviving is you have to keep doing it. Every. Single. Day. You never beat the thing that breaks you, not really. It owns you. It's always with you, no matter what. It becomes a part of you. Like skin. Like broken skin.

Like scar tissue.

The night Giovanni Santa Maria stalked into my life, I knew it was happening again. My life on repeat. The past reappearing.

Sunshine. That's what he calls me.

I'm anything but, though.

He's a powerful man. A ruthless one. One more dangerous than any I've battled before. But I will battle. It's in my nature.

Just as it's in his to win.

He'll take my body. He already has.

But I fucked up and he saw inside my soul, and now, he wants that too.

He likes to watch me. Likes to pull me apart and see the damage inside. I know men like him. They like the chase. They want you to run. To fight. It gets them off.

He's wrong if he thinks he can break me, though. I'm already broken and the thing with survivors is we have nothing to lose.

And I'll give him the fight of his life before I let him steal my soul.

1

EMILIA

I love living in the city, but parking is pretty much always a pain in the ass.

The rain has tapered off, leaving that sticky, steamy humidity behind. It would almost be better if it wouldn't rain, but this July has been stifling.

I climb the stairs up to the outer door of the townhouse and shake out my ring of keys as I balance two grocery bags and my large tote. There are six apartments in this building, one on each floor. I'm lucky to have the top floor because it comes with a rooftop terrace. I just have to remember that it makes up for the six flights of stairs I have to climb daily. Although I hate going to the gym, so this is usually my excuse not to.

It's almost nine at night. I'm later than usual. The light goes on as soon as I step on the sixth-floor landing. It's the motion detector, and for some reason, tonight, it makes me jump. Then again, I've been jumpy all day.

My heels click on the hardwood floor as I make my way to my apartment. It's just my door and one other on this floor, a janitor's closet. Looking over the top of the bags I'm holding, I find the right key and slip it into the lock, hear the click, and feel the familiar weight of the lock turning. That's usually enough to reassure me. To tell me I'm safe. But tonight, it's not, and when I push the door open, it takes me a moment to register that a light is on. The reading lamp over the armchair. It casts a soft glow and is my favorite place to sit.

Except tonight, someone is already sitting in it.

My heart races. Still holding the stupid bags, I look at the huge man in my chair. He's looking at me, and he's incredibly relaxed. Almost smiling, even. He's beautiful, disarmingly so, and impeccably dressed in a black suit. The light bounces off the gold of his cuff links as he brings his glass to his lips.

I take a step back. The overhead lights go on, and I bump into someone behind me. I turn. Another man, also in a dark suit. He's big too, but he doesn't quite look at me. Just makes sure I know I won't be leaving just yet.

"Hope you don't mind that I helped myself to a drink," says the man in the chair. His voice is a deep timbre.

I'm not looking at him. I'm counting the others, three that I can see, standing in various places throughout my apartment. All are well dressed. All looking somewhere in my direction but not quite at me. None but the one in the chair, that is. And his gaze penetrates to my very marrow.

The door clicks closed behind me. I turn my head to look and see one of the suits blocking it, his hands folded in front of him. He's a soldier. I recognize soldiers. There's something in their stance, in the look in their eyes. And these guys are high-level. Whoever the man in my chair is, he's important.

"It's good stuff."

I turn back around when he speaks and watch as he

swallows the last of the amber liquid in one of my tumblers. Ice clinks against the crystal. It's such a pretty sound. A familiar one. Reminds me of my dad and me sitting in his study as he drank his whiskey.

But there's no comfort in that sound today.

The man is still watching me. I'm not sure he's taken his eyes off me since I walked inside. And his expression, it's intense. Like he's trying to figure something out.

He rises to his feet, gives a nod. "Help the lady with her bags."

Another suit comes toward me. I step to the side, but there's nowhere to go. For some reason, I'm clutching the bags like they're a shield. But a moment later, he takes them from me and sets the groceries on the large kitchen island, its white marble veined with gold. It's what separates the kitchen from the rest of the open floor plan living and dining space.

I hear the sound of liquid being poured and watch the man's back—the one who's obviously in charge—as he refills his glass. He approaches me with a second one. He takes me in, his dark eyes roaming my face, my body. He's not smiling anymore. He's big, maybe a good foot taller than me. Even with my three-inch heels, I don't think the top of my head comes to his shoulder. And he's powerfully built. His suit fits him perfectly, stretched tight over broad shoulders and thick arms. I stupidly wonder if it's custom-made.

"Here," he says, holding out one of the tumblers.

I don't move. This isn't my first rodeo. It's not the first time I've been taken by surprise in my own home. I don't think he works for my brother, though. He's no soldier. He's too elegant. Too beautiful. Too much in control.

And I can't see him bowing to my brother—or any man.

My hand shakes when I reach out to take the tumbler,

and I know he sees it too. "Who are you?" I ask. "What do you want?" How does my voice sound so calm?

He sips from his glass and waits for me to do the same. I take the smallest sip. I don't drink whiskey often. I don't really like it. When I do drink it, it's only to try to recapture a fading memory.

"Sit down, Ms. Estrella," he says, rolling the r, watching my face as he says my name. My real name.

I swallow. "It's Larrea. I'm Em Larrea. You have the wrong—"

"I'm not a fool, Emilia." He gestures with a tilt of his head toward the couch.

I look at all the men standing there, and as if they're not enough, a toilet flushes and, moments later, another man walks out of my bathroom. I'm outnumbered. Even if I could get to the kitchen, I'm sure they're all armed and much faster than me.

But I'm not a pushover. I'll fight. I'll claw out their eyes if I have to, but I'll fight because not fighting makes you a victim. An accomplice, even. I am neither. I will never be again.

Although them thinking me docile will only work in my favor. I walk over to the couch and perch on the middle cushion.

He nods and resumes his seat in my armchair. He swirls ice around his glass before taking a sip, but he never once takes his eyes off me.

"You look very different than your brother. Aren't you supposed to be twins?"

I was right. He doesn't work for Alessandro, or he'd never be asking that question.

"Who are you?"

"I'm Giovanni Santa Maria."

Italian. So my guess is mafia. Are they gentler than the cartels? I don't think so.

"What do you want?"

"Information."

"I hardly think I have information that would be of value to you," I say, swallowing a mouthful of my drink and rising to my feet.

The moment I do, two soldiers step forward, each with one hand disappearing into his jacket. Reaching for their guns, no doubt. My heart is racing, but I remind myself they can't hear that. I stop when they move, but Giovanni puts up a hand to halt them. I can see him watching me. It's unsettling the way he does that. Like he's looking for something.

"I'm hungry," I finally turn to him to say. "Do you mind?"

"Go ahead."

I'm pretty sure I wouldn't be able to get a single bite of food down, but I need to get to the kitchen.

I feel his eyes burn into my back as I make my way across the room and around the island. My heels click along the hardwood. I keep my focus on the task of unpacking the groceries, taking out a box of pasta, a jar of sauce, a baguette, a bottle of wine, and several of water. I fold the paper bags and eye the drawer where I keep my pistol, but I don't reach for it just yet. Instead, I tuck the bags into the cupboard beneath the sink and take a water glass from the draining rack. I open one of the bottles and pour myself a glass. Only then do I return my attention to the man in the chair.

He's quiet and patient and hasn't taken his eyes off me for one second. I know instantly not to underestimate him. He's studying me. I wonder what he's learning. One thing I know not to do is mistake his silence for weakness. This man is as dangerous as he is devastatingly beautiful.

He stands, and it takes all I have not to visibly shudder.

As he walks toward the island, I turn to find a pot, one with a long handle, fill it with water, put it on the stove, and turn it on.

"You need to salt the water," he says when I pick up the jar of sauce and struggle to twist the lid off. My hands are sweaty, though, and I have to wipe them on my skirt before trying again. Failing again.

A moment later, he's beside me, too close, and taking up entirely too much space. Using up too much of the oxygen in the room. One side of his mouth seems to be in a constant smirk, and I notice his gaze slip to my neck momentarily and wonder if he can see my pulse. If he knows how hard my heart is beating.

How scared I am. Because the calm, it's a facade.

But he just smiles and holds out his hand.

I look at it, confused, but he reaches for the jar of sauce I'm holding. When his fingers touch mine, there's almost an audible spark of electricity.

It takes me a minute to shift my gaze from his big hands back up to his eyes. He's still steadily watching me, and it's unnerving. He takes the jar and an instant later, there's a *pop*. He smiles and holds out both the lid and the jar to me.

I take them from him. "Thank you."

"You should make your own. It's not hard and much better than that crap."

"I'm fine." I turn my back to pour the contents of the jar into a pot and watch as the pasta water begins to boil. Another weapon if I need one. Two. But I'm hoping I won't need them.

I return my attention to him.

"What information do you want? What is it you think I

know?" I finally ask. Because I need to ask them to leave. I hope that they will.

"You're awfully calm for having a crew of armed men in your apartment," he comments.

I have no response.

"Curious."

He's studying me again, memorizing me. Reading my mind? Whatever he's doing, it's unsettling, his gaze unnerving.

"I have business with your brother, Alessandro. I want to know where he is."

Did my brother really think he could screw with this guy? I'm not even involved in the family business, and I know not to fuck with him.

"I'm sorry, but you came to the wrong place. I don't know anything about Alessandro's whereabouts. We don't keep in touch."

"Hmm." He's scrutinizing me again. "You aren't close to your twin brother? Isn't that how twins are? I mean, don't you have some sort of radar or something?"

I lean against the counter. I'm close to the drawer where my gun is, but I need to be careful. I'll have only one chance, and I'm still hoping he'll leave.

"No, there's no such thing as twin radar. At least not with us. Alessandro and I aren't close. I know nothing about his business or any cartel business for that matter. I left that world when my father was killed. Even when he was alive, I was never a part of it."

He sighs. "Well, that's too bad."

He turns his back. I hear the water beginning to boil and glance over at the pot. Not yet, though. Not yet. He takes a few steps away, makes a point of turning a circle as if to take in the apartment.

"So you mean to tell me your job as an event coordinator at a tiny little hotel pays for all this? Quite the cushy job you've got there."

He's done his homework. Naive to think he wouldn't have.

"I'm a manager, and the tiny little hotel is an exclusive boutique hotel. But my expenses aren't your concern. I told you, I don't know anything about Alessandro's business or whereabouts. There's nothing I can help you with. I'd like you to leave now. Please," I say, adding in that please as an afterthought.

He cocks his head to the side. "Touchy about the money, huh?"

"It's none of your business. Please, get out."

"Or what?"

The water is boiling harder, and when I look over to the stove, I see the tomato sauce sputtering, leaving red-orange stains on the pristine marble. I hate messes. I hate them.

I walk over to the stove and adjust the heat on the sauce, then open the box of pasta and throw in a handful. I put the lid on the pot then walk back over to the drawer that houses my gun, which is near the sink, and rinse my hands. I pick up the towel to dry them. We're watching each other. I'm waiting, though. I'm waiting for the water in the pot to boil over, and, right on time, I hear it, the hissing as it falls onto the stove, the gurgling sound of the lid as it vibrates, and I watch Giovanni do exactly what I think he'll do. He goes over to it to take off the lid and turn down the heat. I think he's making some comment about my cooking skills, but my ears are ringing, and I don't quite hear it because I'm opening the drawer and my hand is closing around the handle of the gun. It's heavy and familiar and still scares the shit out of me. Just as I aim it at him, five soldiers are aiming their weapons at me, the deafening sound of guns being cocked bouncing off the walls.

Giovanni casually turns around, his dark eyes—they're darkest green, I realize. Not black, like I'd thought. His expression hasn't changed. If he's surprised, he doesn't let on, but I suspect he's not.

"Get out. Now," I say, cocking my gun when he takes a step toward me. It takes all I have not to retreat.

"And here for a minute, I thought you were just an innocent girl caught in an ugly world."

"I'm not a girl. I'm a woman."

His gaze sweeps over me. "I can see that," he says, and I think he expected my retort.

"I'll shoot," I say, this time taking that step backward when he keeps coming toward me. "I mean it."

His smile widens, and he stops, putting his arms up in mock surrender. Without looking away from me, he gives an order to his men. "Put your weapons away, gentlemen. Emilia is just protecting herself against this perceived invasion."

"My name is Em. And it's not perceived. You broke into my home."

"Not true. Building manager was kind enough to lend me a spare key."

"What?"

He ignores me. "Emil was your father, right? Strange he named his daughter after him and not his son and successor."

"My family is none of your business. Get out, because if you think I won't shoot, you're wrong."

His smile vanishes. "You and I both know you won't, so go ahead and put down your gun, Emilia. I won't ask twice."

I swallow. Somehow, he's walked me backward far

enough that my back is against the wall. When did that happen?

"Please go. I won't ask again either," I say, nerves making my voice quaver.

"All right, then, we'll do it your way."

Something moves in my periphery, distracting me, and that's all it takes for him to have one of his hands around both of mine and the other around my throat. He pushes my arms downward and pins me to the wall. When he squeezes my wrists, the pistol drops to the floor. It goes off, and I scream.

Giovanni keeps me pinned there, pressing his body against mine, almost shielding me with it. He's huge, and I can't move. My heart seems to be trying to beat its way out of my chest. All I can do is feel his hard shoulder against my face, smell a dark hint of aftershave while I try to hold back weak, frightened tears.

"Christ," he says a second later, backing off me. "Fucking amateurs." He steps backward and picks up the pistol. "You need a Drop-Safety on this. How old is it?" He's inspecting it, turning it this way and that.

But I can't speak because his men have their guns out again and they're all aimed at me. Giovanni shakes his head, empties my pistol of bullets, and tucks it and the ammunition into his pocket.

"That's mine."

"You're going to hurt yourself with it."

"I'm not an idiot."

"Really? And you thought it was a good idea to point a loaded weapon at me with five of my men surrounding you? That doesn't seem like something an intelligent person would do, *Em*." He puts the emphasis on my name, and it pisses me off.

"Fuck you. I know you, and I know your kind. Get out of my house."

"Ballsy, considering your situation."

He steps to me again, this time any laughter is wiped away from his face as he closes his hands around my arms, rubs them, then squeezes. He watches me as he does, and it takes everything I have to stand still, to keep silent while he hurts me. This is just a sneak peek of that hurt. A preview of what he can do. I know that.

"Honestly, though, I prefer women with a little fire. They're much more fun in bed." He leans in close to say the next part. "They're the dirty girls."

One of his men chuckles. It wasn't a whisper at all.

He pulls back, and I look up at him. He moves a hand toward my neck and sets two fingers on my throbbing pulse. He doesn't comment. Just wants me to know he knows.

"I want to talk to your brother. I don't care what you have to do to get ahold of him, but you do it and pass my message along. It'll be in your best interest that he turns up by next week, understand?"

I swallow, processing his words.

What I'm seeing here, this cool, collected side of him—it's his most dangerous side. I get the feeling he's at his worst when he's speaking calmly like this.

"Eyes up here," he says, giving me a shake. I realize I'd shifted my gaze downward.

I blink and look up at him.

"Do you understand, Emilia?"

I nod.

"You're a big girl. Use your words."

I fist my hands.

He raises his eyebrows.

"Yes, I understand," I spit.

"Good. Because I'd hate to have to hurt you." He releases me, cocks his head to the side, then turns to the stove. "I think you burned dinner."

I look over too. He's right. I can smell that the sauce is stuck to the pot.

"That's too bad," he says, walking back toward me. He reaches out. I flinch, but he just tucks a hair that had come loose of my tight bun behind my ear and gives me a charming smile, baring his white teeth. "I'll be seeing you again, Emilia Estrella."

And with that, he walks out the door, his men following him. I slump against the wall and clutch my stomach and find the bullet hole in the baseboard, the one left by my gun when I dropped it.

I may have grown up in a cartel family, but this is the closest I've ever been to death.

2

GIOVANNI

Emilia Estrella isn't what I expect.

"Keep a man on her. I want to know about everyone she has contact with," I say once we're on the street. I look up and down the pretty, wealthy Upper East Side neighborhood. No way she lives here on a hotel manager's salary. I take one more glance at the townhouse, at the windows on the top floor.

"Yes, sir," Vincent says. He's standing beside my car, holding the door open.

"Make sure it's not some idiot. And if she meets with that piece-of-shit brother of hers, you bring them both to me."

"I'll take care of it, sir."

I get into the car, take the key to her apartment out of my pocket, and slide it onto my own key ring. I want access to Emilia Larrea-Estrella, and it's not just because of her brother. But now isn't the time to think about that other thing, even if I can't get the image of those strange, striking serpentine eyes out of my head. I should have been better prepared. It would have been easy enough to get one fucking photo of her. If I'd done that, I wouldn't be sitting here dissecting this right now because I'd have been prepared.

She's not my ghost. I know that. But fuck me, when I first saw her, it took me back.

What she did, standing up to me—most people would cower. I knew she had a plan the moment she went into the kitchen. I still wonder if she'd have had the guts to use the pot of boiling water as a weapon. She seemed pretty calm, but they're usually the most dangerous kind. If you can stay calm in a situation like the one she just experienced, it means you've seen some shit very close to home. I'm curious about that shit.

Or hell, maybe I just want to fuck her.

I reach into my pocket, retrieve my cell phone, and dial Dominic Benedetti, my cousin and the head of the Benedetti family to which I'm loyal. He answers on the second ring.

"Find that son of a bitch yet?"

"Not yet, but I met the sister tonight."

"And?"

"I think she's telling the truth about not knowing where he is, but I've tasked her with finding him. Gave her some incentive to do so."

Dominic chuckles. "Killian Black is a good resource, too. He has a man, Hugo Drake, he's also reliable. I thought with old man Estrella's assassination, we were done with this shit, but the son is worse than the father."

"Isn't that always the case?"

He's silent for a minute, and I think about what I just said. How true it is for him and for me.

"You sound like my brother Salvatore," Dominic says.

Salvatore is Dominic's older brother. "I'll take that as a compliment."

"I want this bastard."

"No more than me. It was me he made the deal with. Me he thinks he'll make a fool of."

"Just make sure you bring him in alive. I plan on doing the killing myself, although I'm guessing there's a fucking line out the door."

It's my turn to chuckle. "I'll keep you posted. I plan on visiting the sister again tomorrow night." I tell myself I'd be doing this even if she didn't look like she does.

"I like your commitment." He understands my meaning.

We hang up just as Vincent pulls into the garage. I don't live too far from Emilia, and my building is about the same size as hers, except that I own all six floors.

I walk up the stairs and into the house, entering via the kitchen. While her apartment has a chic, feminine design, the decor in my house is completely modern. I make my way straight into my study to boot up my laptop. Tonight, I want to read all I can about the Estrella cartel, about Emil Estrella's untimely death. And Emilia Estrella, who all but disappeared after that night.

I know enough about Alessandro. He's a liar. A thief. And an idiot if he thinks he can double cross me or the Benedetti family. A fucking imbecile.

But it's not him I'm interested in tonight. It's Emil Estrella's pretty, fiery daughter. The girl who looks like my past come back to haunt me.

The next night, I'm waiting outside The Clementine, the luxury boutique hotel where Emilia works. It's a little after seven, and I know she's going home right around now. I called in and checked her schedule. I also know that last night, after I left, she went out for a run, even though the rain had picked up again. The man I had on her lost her as he wasn't on foot, and I'm curious where she went because she was gone for over two hours. Did she meet with her brother? Does she know where that little snake is hiding and keeping his secret? I would have said no after my first meeting with her, but maybe I'm wrong.

I've doubled the men on her, one on foot and one by car. I'll find out soon enough.

And right now, I don't want to think about that because Em Larrea, as she's known here, just walked out the side door of the hotel and is heading to her car. Seeing her again is strange, puts me off balance. At least momentarily.

She's not your fucking ghost.

I know that. I buried that ghost years ago.

With a shake of my head, I banish those thoughts and focus on her. She's wearing a similar outfit to what she wore the other night, a beige two-piece, close-cut suit. She removes the jacket to reveal a ruffled silk blouse beneath, and that pencil skirt is making it hard to look away as she shimmies her tight little ass past my car and toward hers. My windows are tinted, so she doesn't see me.

I open my door as soon as she gets to her car but before she's dug out her keys.

"Emilia."

She stops, and I can see from how her back stiffens that she recognizes my voice.

I take a few steps, and although it's well past seven o'clock, the sun is still too hot in the sky. She turns slowly. I'm wearing dark sunglasses, but hers are in her hand. She's squinting up at me. Her eyes are even prettier in the sunlight with gold specks lighting up that strange shade of green. Her dark hair is up in that same tight bun as last night. I have the urge to pull it out, to see it spilling down her back and framing her pretty face.

"You always leave work so late?" I ask.

"What the hell are you doing here?"

"That's not the warmest welcome when I've gone out of my way to come see you."

She wants to say something, but her gaze moves to just over my shoulder, where I hear two women talking. I glance back at the employees who are leaving. They're younger, maybe late teens, and in uniforms. Bar staff, probably.

"This is my workplace."

"Would you rather I wait for you at your apartment?"

"What? No. What do you want? I have a week, you said so. I told you, I don't keep in touch with—"

"I know what I said."

The two girls quiet as they near their car, which is parked a few spaces away. I can see Emilia is uncomfortable, but that will only help my case.

"You shouldn't be here. They don't know who my family is here," she says, her voice quieter.

"Then let's go," I say, gesturing to my car, where Vincent is standing watch.

"Where?"

"Dinner."

"I have plans."

"What plans?"

"None of your business. What's this about? Really?"

The door opens again, and someone comes running from the hotel, calling out to her. "Em! Oh, I'm glad I caught you."

When she reaches us, she stops, as if just now realizing I'm here, and fumbles for words when she sees me.

"Sorry, I didn't know you were with someone."

"I'm not," Emilia says.

"Oh." The girl looks from her to me and back.

"What is it?" Emilia asks her.

"The file for the Ragoni engagement party. I have some updated notes, and I didn't have a chance to get them changed out before you left. Here you go."

She hands over a folder to Em. It is clear she is waiting for an introduction. It's kind of funny, watching Emilia try to pretend I'm invisible.

"Thank you." There's an awkward pause, and I clear my throat.

"I'm Giovanni Santa Maria," I say. "A friend of *Em*. I believe we spoke on the phone earlier?"

"You what?" Emilia asks.

"Katy, isn't it?" The girl nods with a huge smile on her face. "Katy here was kind enough to give me your schedule for the week."

I see Emilia look at the girl, see the disbelief in her eyes, but Katy's oblivious. She's busy staring up at me.

"Oh. Mr. Santa Maria," she says. Her cheeks flush red, and she holds out her hand. "I'm glad I could be of help."

I turn back to Emilia. "So, we'll pick up your car later. Ready?"

Katy stands there and watches us as Vincent opens the back door.

Emilia hesitates, but I know she's not going to make a big deal out of it. Not in front of the girl. A moment later, she walks over to the sedan and climbs into the back, the high slit of her skirt giving me a glimpse of one slender thigh.

"Well, have a nice night, Katy."

"Thank you. You too, Mr. Santa Maria. Bye, Em." She gives an awkward wave. Emilia looks straight ahead.

When Vincent pulls away, I notice the girl is still standing there, watching.

"She seems quite anxious."

"That was unnecessary. You can't just show up at my work and...bully me into having dinner with you."

"I didn't exactly bully you. I invited you. I'm offended, Emilia."

"My name is Em."

"No, it's not. It only became Em a few years ago. After your father's death, if I understand correctly." Her lips draw into a tight line. She's obviously taken aback by my knowledge.

"How do you know that?"

"I make it my business to know about the people I do business with."

"We don't do business together."

I shrug a shoulder. "I assume you like Italian, since you were attempting to cook it last night." She shifts her attention to the window, and I can't see her face.

"Where are we going?"

"A little place I know just outside the city. Beautiful views and delicious food." She looks at me, opens her mouth to speak. "Don't worry. I'll take you back to get your car after dinner."

"Why do you want to have dinner with me?"

"Because you make me curious."

She doesn't reply to this but watches the view outside her window as Vincent drives us to Trattoria Giacomo, one of the few remaining places near the city that tourists haven't discovered.

Vincent parks the car. The lot is full, but there's always a table for me. I climb out and walk around to her side to open the door.

"I hope you're hungry."

She reaches back inside for her jacket.

"Leave it," I say. "I like you better without it."

She gives me a glare and makes a point of putting the jacket back on even in the stifling heat.

"Suit yourself." With a hand at her low back, I guide her to the entrance where we're greeted by the owner. He takes us to a table on the deck outside, where we can see the view of the city but still have privacy.

"Thank you, Giacomo," I say as I pull out a chair for my guest.

She sits, and I order a bottle of white wine. Emilia picks up her menu right away.

"I suggest the Spaghetti Vongole to start and any of the fish for dinner."

She doesn't reply. When Giacomo comes back with the wine, he pours for both of us. We order, and I'm happy to see she orders what I suggested.

"Good choice," I say as I pick up my glass.

She picks up hers as well and takes a sip without touching it to mine first.

"You're being quite rude."

"You broke into my house with five of your men and threatened to hurt me if I don't help you find my brother to do God knows what to him, and you think I'm being *rude*? We're not friends. We're not even acquaintances."

"Okay, you make a point. How about we call a truce, then? Just for dinner."

"I don't understand why we have to have dinner at all."

I shrug a shoulder. I want to seem casual. But looking at her in this light, when she's squinting into the waning sun and I can see the flecks of gold in her eyes, it makes me remember so many things. "Like I said, you make me curious. And for the record, I don't want to hurt you."

"But for the record, you will if you have to."

I take a moment to study her before speaking. "The keyword there is "if." Who are you hiding from, Emilia?"

"I'm not," she answers too quickly, then clears her throat. "I'm not in hiding."

"They why did you legally change your name to your grandmother's maiden name."

"How do you know that?"

"I mean, finding you wasn't easy, but it wasn't that hard either. You should have used an anonymous name. Like Jones or Smith. That would have made it much harder, although not impossible."

"I'm not hiding from anyone. I changed my name because I don't want to be associated with the cartel. I want a simple life. I don't want anything to do with my brother or his business. So you can understand why I'm not that nice to you."

The food comes, and I wait until the waiter is gone before speaking.

"You know, family isn't something you just decide you're no longer part of. The farther you try to run, the tighter you're tethered."

She's good at masking her thoughts, but this makes her pause. I see it, at least momentarily. I wonder, though, if it's something in her own life or how the comment relates to me that's made her stop. That's turned the tables, making her study me now. A moment later, she picks up her glass and drinks more of her wine.

"You're making assumptions about me when you don't know me."

"Isn't running what you're doing, though? You claim

you're not in hiding, but you disappeared after your father's death. Never returned to school. No one saw or heard from you again. You've since legally changed your last name. The company you work for has no idea who you really are. I get the feeling you keep everyone at a distance."

"What's your point?"

I keep my attention on her while draining the last of my wine.

"Or do you just want to try and get under my skin? You won't. I've dealt with your kind before."

"My kind?"

"Arrogant egomaniacs."

"Wow. And how do you come to that conclusion about me?"

"I knew it the instant I saw you. You're a bully. You expect everyone to cower at your feet. You use whatever means necessary to get what you want. Me, for example. This whole thing." She gestures to the table.

"My patience is wearing thin, Emilia."

That checks her, and she turns her attention to her plate and rolls spaghetti onto her fork, only glancing at me from beneath thick lashes.

But she's too stubborn to drop it. "Isn't it true, though?"

"Where did you go last night?"

I can see she's surprised by the question.

"Are you having me followed?"

"I wouldn't want you to disappear like before. You seem to be pretty good at it. Did you see your brother?"

"No. I went for a run. I already told you I don't know where he is."

I lean in close. "If it turns out you do—"

"I don't—"

"He won't be the only one I punish," I finish as if she

hasn't spoken.

Her eyes search mine, perhaps weighing my words, trying to figure out if I mean them. I do. She can be sure of that.

"How about that truce?" I ask.

Reluctantly, she nods.

There's something strange about her. Something different than I expect. She's afraid of me. She's trying to be brave, to put on a show, but she's scared, which is normal, considering. But there's more—there's almost an acceptance, for all her fight. A submission. A sadness just beneath the surface, quiet but deep. For some reason, I want to touch that darkness.

"Let your hair down." I don't know why I want this. No, that's a lie. I do.

"What?"

"Your hair."

She touches it, then, she again surprises me by pulling the jeweled clip out and letting it fall down over her shoulders. She combs the long, thick waves back with her fingers, and there's a softness to her when I see her like this. The dark hair with her olive skin and those green eyes, not to mention the red lips, swollen and like a heart.

A broken heart.

"Why don't you have a boyfriend?"

She's pushing food around her plate, and the only sign I have that she's surprised by my question is the momentary pause in the twirling of spaghetti onto her fork. She tilts her head so she's looking at me.

"If you think I'm going to fuck you after dinner, think again."

Rebellion and submission are warring inside her, each one equal. She's cautious, because she knows she'll lose any fight with me. She's choosing her words and her battles.

I grin.

"Well, I would like to fuck you after dinner, but I wasn't assuming it was a given." Long minutes of silence pass as we eat. "Aren't you curious what Alessandro did?"

She puts the last forkful of pasta into her mouth and sits back, chewing thoughtfully as she picks up her wine and drains her glass. "This was good," she says. "I'm glad I ordered it. Thank you for recommending it."

"You're a strange girl, Emilia Estrella."

"Larrea. It's officially Larrea now. Emilia…Em Larrea."

"Then you're a strange girl, Emilia Larrea."

"Sorry to disappoint you."

"I'm not disappointed."

She studies me as a waiter clears our plates and brings a different wine for the main course.

"So why don't you have a boyfriend? You're a very pretty girl."

"Maybe I have a girlfriend."

"You don't."

"Why don't *you* have a girlfriend, Giovanni? Or do you, and does she know you're here with me?"

"No girlfriend. I don't cheat." I finish my last bite and set my utensils down before wiping my mouth.

I think she's surprised by my comment. "Well, good for you," she says, finishing her food. She checks her watch. "I have an early day…"

"Don't worry, I'll get you home before you turn into a pumpkin."

My cell phone rings just then, the interruption annoying me. I check the display. It's Janet. That doesn't usually mean a good thing.

"Excuse me," I say, standing as I swipe the screen to answer and walk around the deck to the back of the restaurant for privacy.

"Giovanni, it's Janet. I'm sorry to bother you. I know—"

"What is it, Janet?" Janet is my father's live-in nurse.

"I just wanted you to know he's been having those dreams again. The nightmares. He's been calling out your name."

"And what do you want me to do about it?"

"He wakes up in an awful sweat, Giovanni." There's a pause, but I don't fill it. "He's an old man, and I worry you'll regret this someday. I know he can forgive you if you can forgive him."

"Tell the doctor to up his meds. That should take care of the nightmares."

"Giovanni—"

"I have to go. Good-bye, Janet."

I hang up before she can say anything more. When I return to our table at the restaurant, Emilia is gone. I think she may be in the bathroom, but then Giacomo comes to me holding a handful of bills.

"She said she had an emergency. Took a taxi I'd called for someone else. She gave me this."

I take the money and assume it's to cover her meal. It's an insult to me. I exhale.

"I'm sorry, I didn't know what to do. I told her to wait, but she simply left."

"It's all right, it's not your fault," I say, my mind distracted. She expects me to chase her. She must know I will. I smile at Giacomo, pat his back. "You have any of your homemade Limoncello?"

3

EMILIA

I'm not sure why I left. It's not like he doesn't know where I live. And I know he'll come after me. In fact, during the ride to pick up my car and then onto my apartment, all I've been doing is worrying about this. His phone call gave me the opportunity to slip away, and I took it without thinking of the consequences.

He's too observant. Too curious. He can't start snooping. What he learns, it could destroy everything.

I hope he finds Alessandro and leaves me alone. He doesn't believe I won't help him with that. I don't ever want to see my brother again. I don't ever want him near me again. But I already know Giovanni is a force to be reckoned with. He won't let me off the hook, and I do believe he will hurt me if he has to.

It's just a matter of choosing which will be worse. Which of the two I am more likely to survive.

When I climb the final staircase to my apartment, I half expect him to be waiting there for me. I'm not sure if I'm relieved or disappointed when he's not.

I unlock my apartment door. I have to remember to

make an appointment with a locksmith to change the locks. I wouldn't be surprised if Giovanni had a key. Hell, maybe I have to move altogether. If he could find me, Alessandro can too. Maybe he already knows where I am.

No, he can't know that. If he did, he'd have come for me.

My keys clang against the bowl on the table by the door where I drop them. The lights are on. I'd left them on this morning. I don't want to be surprised again. I walk into the kitchen, pour myself a glass of water, and stand by the counter, watching the door as I drink it, waiting. Waiting for him.

What he said keeps repeating in my head.

"Family isn't something you just decide you're no longer part of. The farther you try to run, the tighter you're tethered."

I lied to Giovanni earlier. I am hiding from my own brother. I took the Larrea name for two reasons. One, I don't think Alessandro would expect me to do so. He'd expect me to do what Giovanni said. Use a name like Jones. But the second reason is more important. I don't want to be a part of the cartel, but that doesn't mean I'm ashamed of who I am. Who my father is. My mother. My grandmother. And making Larrea my legal name, in a way, it makes me feel closer to them.

I'm not running or hiding from my past. Just my brother.

When a full hour passes, and he doesn't come, I wonder if I'm wrong. If he's not going to come after me tonight. Maybe he'd had enough after that dinner. I'm sure I didn't provide the challenge he expected, the fire he so liked. I'd ordered what he suggested, let my hair down when he asked, and our conversation had to be about as enjoyable for him as it was for me. So maybe fucking me has lost its appeal.

I double-check the lock on the door before heading into

my bedroom. It's large and beautiful. The whole apartment is, with gorgeous hardwood floors, heavy, ornate doors, intricate crown molding, and chic but comfortable furniture. The colors are all muted, white and beige with gold tones and hints of color in shades of softest green.

I slip off my jacket, and when I open the closet doors, the lights go on automatically. Here, too, everything is neat and in its place. The housekeeper comes twice a week and knows how I like things. I lay my suit jacket, skirt, and blouse in the dry-cleaning bag. She'll take care of it at the end of the week. My shoes I place in their cubbyhole among the rest. I touch the shiny heel, stand back, and look at them, then look around the closet. Here, too, the colors are muted, subtle, for the most part.

Stripping off my bra and panties, I drop them into the hamper and make my way back through the bedroom and into the bathroom. The marble in here matches that in the kitchen, and the fixtures are brushed gold to pick up on the lines in the marble. I look at myself in the mirror. My face is blank of expression as I run the water and wrap my long hair back up into a clip to wash off my makeup. I then walk over to the shower and switch it on, glancing back at my reflection as the water begins to steam, looking at the lines that crisscross the whole of my back. I've gotten good at this. I don't feel anything when I look at them anymore. Not pain. Not shame. Not betrayal. Not fear.

They're ugly, the lines. Some of them, at least. I touch the one at my shoulder. Thick scar tissue feels bumpy beneath my finger. I press against it, testing. I don't feel a thing.

I make myself look every time. I make myself remember every day. And I'm grateful that at least he didn't cut my face. My back I can hide.

I step into the shower for a quick rinse, then climb out, reach for one of the lush towels folded on the rack, and wrap it around myself, liking the faint scent of detergent that clings to it. Clean. I like clean.

At the bathroom door, I stop to listen, wondering if he's here now. Asking myself if I want him to be or if I'm disappointed when I open the door and find that I'm still alone.

Drying off, I walk to the window, open it a crack. Even though the air-conditioning is running, I need the noise of the city to sleep. It's comforting somehow. Like I'm not alone. I climb beneath the covers and switch out the light. Somehow, I never really have a hard time falling asleep. I should, considering, but I don't.

———

Silk tickles my skin, and it takes me a moment to realize it's the blanket sliding off me. I reach for it, still half-asleep, but when I hear a "Tsk-tsk," my body goes rigid and my eyelids fly open. In the light coming through the sheer window curtains, I see the outline of a man. He's huge and standing at the foot of my bed. I know it's him. I recognize his voice, his build. His aftershave.

"You left before coffee."

I sit up, or try to, but he grabs my ankle and tugs on it and stops me.

I want to cover myself, but the blanket is out of reach, so I lie there, naked. Giovanni smiles and his gaze slowly travels over me.

"Were you expecting me, or do you always sleep naked?"

I kick the leg he's got, but when I do, he tugs me down the bed. Turning me slightly, he slaps my ass hard.

"Ow!" He's not smiling when I look back at him, my hand covering the spot he just hit.

"You deserve more than that."

I realize he's not wearing his suit jacket anymore but has his shirt sleeves rolled halfway up his powerful forearms. I wonder how long he's been here watching me. There's a dusting of dark hair on his arms, and the only jewelry he's wearing is a heavy, expensive watch.

"What are you doing here?"

"Oh, come on, don't pretend to be surprised. You knew I'd come."

He lets me go, and I scramble back up the bed, sit up on my knees, and grab the pillow to cover myself. Giovanni walks patiently around the bed, and as he does, I mirror his movements. He switches on the light. I see he's grinning. Moving much faster than I expect, he grabs the pillow from me and tosses it across the room.

"What are you doing?"

"I didn't get to have dessert," he says, placing one knee on the bed, catching me as I try to scramble off, tugging me into his chest. "Now lie down and spread those beautiful legs, so I can get my dessert."

"You're a freak!" I scream, shoving at his chest, but he only laughs it off and tosses me on my back onto the bed like I weigh nothing. I flip over onto my belly to get away, but he easily catches me by the ankle and tugs me flat and this time, presses a knee to my back. I know I fucked up because he stops. I hear him suck in a breath—or maybe that was me—because I know what he's looking at.

It takes me a minute to turn my head to look over my shoulder and see his eyes, see the serious expression there as he eyes my back, the ugly crisscrossing of lines.

"Get off me."

He drags his gaze to mine. "No," he says, as he keeps me in place with his knee on my back. He just studies me for a long time. Not touching, not moving, Just taking in every inch of my back. And I feel myself shrinking. Feel his power over me growing.

I make a sound, wriggle beneath him, but he easily keeps me pinned and ignores me as he trails his fingers along the thin silvery lines that mark me where the skin broke, where my back was opened, and I feel my face burning because it's private, this thing, it's more private than any part of me. And it shows my weakness. And I don't want him to see it. I don't want him to know it's there at all and that I fucked up.

But then he meets my gaze again, and that grin is back, although forced, I think, at least at first, until it isn't, and somehow, the wickedness of it is a relief.

"You're going to have to tell me that story sometime," he says, then flips me back over and slips off the bed to kneel on the floor, pulling me toward him, spreading my legs, his thick arms beneath my knees, hands gripping my thighs as he roughly brings me to his face.

"What are you—"

I gasp, my hands fisting the sheets as his mouth closes around my pussy and his hot, wet tongue licks me, tastes me, draws back to look at me, then meets my eyes and takes my swollen clit into his mouth and sucks and that sound, those sighs, that moaning, it's coming from me.

He grins, and I close my eyes. Giovanni pulls me tighter to him, devouring me, the scruff on his jaw a rough contrast to the softness of his lips, his tongue, and it feels so good. Too fucking good.

My eyes fly open, and I try to pull myself free, but he tightens his grip.

Fuck, I'm going to come, and he knows it. He can hear it, hear my whimpers, my moans, and when he next takes my clit between his lips and sucks, I do. I cry out, and it takes me moments to come. Fuck, I come so hard I'm bucking against his face, and I hate him and I'm lost and it feels so fucking good that I can't do anything but feel, feel it, feel him, let myself go. Let myself come.

When I open my eyes again, he's releasing me, rising to stand. His eyes, so dark now, are locked on mine. He wipes the back of his hand across his mouth and he's looming over me, and I just lie there, limp. Hollowed out, like he carved out a piece of me.

Planting his hands on either side of me, he leans over and brings his face to mine, inhaling, almost like an animal, like a predator scenting his prey. I swallow, and when he touches his lips to mine, I open for him. But he doesn't kiss me, and he doesn't close his eyes. Instead, he takes my lower lip between his teeth and bites, not hard, not hard enough to break skin.

I feel him against me, his hardness at my sex, and I want him again. I want him inside me. I want to come with him inside me.

And I know from the look on his face when he pulls back that he knows it too.

"Your pussy's greedy, Emilia."

He straightens. My legs are half hanging off the bed, and he's standing between them.

I look at him, confused.

"You don't get to come twice, though. Not after how you behaved tonight." He slaps my hip before he turns and heads toward the door, but stops just before he gets there, and I sit up.

He retraces his steps and, reaching into his pocket, he

takes out a stack of bills. He sets them on the nightstand, then reaches for me and grips my jaw, his fingers digging into me as he tilts my face upward.

He's firm when he speaks. Like he's just remembered his annoyance with me. "You don't pay for dinner when I take you out. You eat, and you say thank-you. And you definitely don't walk out. Understand?"

"And then what? I spread my legs?" My heart is racing. I shouldn't challenge this man. I know better.

But he's ready for my comment. I think he likes it from the narrowing of his eyes, the grin on his face.

"That's ideal. Although like I said at dinner, I didn't expect to sleep with you. Dinner wasn't about me buying your pussy. Because that'd make you a whore, wouldn't it? And I don't think you're a whore, are you, Emilia?"

Before I can answer, he releases me. I'm not even up on my useless, shaky legs before he's gone. Out of the bedroom and out of the apartment. I hear the door open and close. Hear the lock turn.

The bastard has a key.

4

GIOVANNI

I swear I can still taste her on my tongue, and fuck if I don't want to go back to her apartment and fuck her raw because my hand just isn't going to do the trick tonight. Coming against the shower wall won't give me the release fucking her tight little cunt will. I want to be inside her. I want to feel her wet pussy squeeze my dick. I want to empty inside her and watch her face as I fill her up. Watch her face when she comes.

But I meant what I said. She doesn't get to come twice when she acts like an idiot.

This girl is a complete mystery. When I first sought her out, I did it because she was my best bet on finding Alessandro Estrella. Her resemblance to the skeleton in my closet caught me unprepared, but that's not what this is about. There's something beneath the surface, that sadness I sensed last night at dinner, that well of darkness inside her. I can't resist it. I don't even want to. For having a big mouth, she has a vulnerability, a quiet courage. Although courage can often lead to stupidity, and I have a feeling she might just be self-destructive enough to go that route.

Is that it? Is she self-destructive?

Or is she smart, hedging her bets, knowing the battles she may have a shot at winning and rolling over for the ones she can't? Because if that's the case, then something happened to her. Something made her like that, broke her, because by nature, she's a fighter. I'd be willing to be my life on that.

And I have a feeling the scars on her back are that something.

The thought makes me angry. To break something wild, it's not right.

The image of those silvery-white lines is burned onto my mind. I've seen some shit. I've done some shit. But her back, it was bad. She was whipped and badly. I can almost see the rage in the hand that held the lash.

I want to know who did it.

I want to know what she did to earn it. If she deserved it.

My gut tells me no and that all roads lead back to one man: Alessandro Estrella.

But I don't know their family history. Why would her own brother do something like that to her? It doesn't make any sense. They're twins. Seriously, aren't twins linked somehow? I have no fucking clue.

The next morning, I'm in my study making calls. The first one I make is to a florist. I order three dozen blood roses sent to her work. I like these. Black and darkest red. Fitting from a mobster to a cartel princess. And even if she is distancing herself from the cartel now, she is still that. A cartel princess. The note attached tells her that Vincent will pick her up at eight for dinner, and if she's good, she'll get to come twice tonight. I'm still smiling at the silence on the florist's end of the line when she took down my message.

That assistant of hers will be spilling about who she

thinks sent them. I don't know why I get a certain pleasure from that. I know Emilia will hate the attention. Will hate anyone poking into her life, nosing around. She's afraid they'll find out who she is, but what I said about family, it's also true in that that you can't run from who you are, and she is an Estrella whether she likes it or not. She can change her name a hundred times, it won't make a single difference.

After the florist, I make a call to Killian Black. He's the owner of Mea Culpa and a man Dominic trusts. He and Hugo Drake. Killian answers on the first ring.

"This is Giovanni Santa Maria."

"Dominic said you'd be calling. What can I do for you, Giovanni?"

"You have surveillance of the meeting with Estrella, correct?" Mea Culpa was where the meeting between myself and Estrella took place. That's when we discussed specifics. He'd brought men with him when he was supposed to have come alone, but I forgave him that. A gesture of goodwill. But no good deed goes unpunished. I should know better.

I know about Killian Black's penchant for recording things. Even though that meeting was off-limits, I have no doubt he has a copy of it somewhere.

He clears his throat. He's not going to lie about it. He may work for Dominic, but he's a force to be reckoned with in his own right. He's not scared of me. I know that, and I respect him for it.

"I want a copy."

"I'll have a copy sent to you this morning."

"The men he brought, I assume you already have names?"

"Would you like that file as well?"

Of course he has files. "Yes."

"There was one complication."

I notice his use of the past tense. "What complication?"

"Estrella had brought four men. Only three are alive."

"And you know why the fourth one isn't?"

"Turned out Hugo knew him from his time in prison."

"Ah." I smile. "Good to know. Let me ask you another question. The sister, Emilia, know anything about her?"

"No. Just that she disappeared after the attack that killed her father. Assumption is that she'd died in the fire too."

"No. She's alive and well. Goes by Larrea now. Em Larrea. See what you can find on those four years she was missing, will you? I'm coming up short."

"Will do. Anything else?"

"That's it. Thank you."

I WOULD COLLECT EMILIA MYSELF BUT FOR THE FACT THAT I'M delayed at a meeting. But when I get a call from Vincent, telling me she isn't at work, that she'd apparently left earlier than expected, I am surprised. I call Katy, her assistant, who recognizes my voice. I can almost see her blushing through the phone. Katy lets me know that Em decided at the last minute to join her birthday outing with several other colleagues and had gone home to change. She promptly invites me to join after mentioning how beautiful and romantic the delivery of roses was. I take down the name of the place and ask her not to mention it to *Em*—Christ, I hate when they call her that—because I want to surprise her.

At midnight, I show up at the club where the party is taking place. Katy's apparently turning twenty-one and wants to celebrate at a new trendy place in town with the worst possible music. Or maybe I'm just too old for this shit.

Vincent and I enter and find the long table in the corner

reserved for Katy and her friends, some of whom look like they must have used fake IDs to get in because no way they're of age, and if they are, they obviously can't hold their liquor.

I scan the dance floor for Emilia and finally spot her across the room at the bar. She's wearing a tight-fitting little black dress that comes up to the nape of her neck—and I know why now—and a pair of high-heeled sandals. Her hair's in that tight bun, although wisps have fallen out around her face. I wonder if she's already been dancing. She takes her drink from the bartender and smiles politely at the idiot who's paying for it. Immediately, my hackles go up.

"Wait outside. We won't be here long," I tell Vincent before making my way to the bar.

She doesn't see me right at first and leans her back against the bar, watching the dancers. The man beside her has his eyes trained on her. My hands fist at the look in his eyes. She's all but ignoring him. Until she spots me, that is. Surprise animates her features, and I give her a tight grin. It feels more like a baring of teeth. I reach the bar and, without hesitation, step between them.

"Emilia."

"Giovanni."

"Um, excuse us," the idiot says in his too-high voice.

I look down at him. "What do you want?" My lips are a hard line.

Emilia throws her drink back and leans over me. "You know what? I changed my mind. Let's dance. It's John, right?"

"James, actually," the idiot corrects. I order a whiskey, fold my arms across my chest, and lean against the bar as I let them walk onto the dance floor.

I watch her move, watch her pick up the beat and raise

her arms over her head and start to dance. It's seductive, her dance. In time with the music, but something so different than every other person around her. I wonder if she's aware how tempting she is.

She only glances at me, but I've got my eyes locked on her. Does that fool think for a second he's even in her fucking league? I'd kill him if it weren't for how pathetic he is.

But when he puts his hands on her hips, it takes all I have not to crush the cheap glass in my hand as I swallow the whiskey and stalk onto the floor. People part to let me through—they must feel the menace coming off me. I don't take my eyes off her for a second. When I reach them, her glance is apprehensive. She knows I'm pissed, but she's testing me.

"Get lost," I tell the idiot, shoving my glass at him as I push him out of the way. He takes the glass because he has no choice. "We're leaving." I take her arm.

"*We* aren't doing anything," she says, planting her heels into the floor.

I stop for a moment, turn to her, and raise my eyebrows.

"I'm here for a party. I want to stay."

"That's too bad." I turn and take two steps.

"Stop. Let me go."

I stop and face her again. "I'm going to give you one chance to walk out of here with your dignity intact, but we *are* leaving. Now." With that warning, I resume my walk. This time when she resists, I stop. "I warned you." I give a shake of my head and then, before she can reply, I wrap my arm around the backs of her thighs and toss her over my shoulder. Someone gasps, and everyone is staring at us now. I know how caveman-like this is but don't give a single fuck.

Emilia is struggling, pounding against my back, but I

just keep moving, holding back when what I really want to do is smack that ass of hers until she obeys. This woman gets under my fucking skin. She provokes me like no other.

"My purse is still in there!"

Once we're out in the parking lot, I set her on her feet beside the car.

"I'm sure Katy will bring it to work for you." I point to the open car door.

"What is wrong with you?"

"I told you that you were being picked up."

"No, that's not how things work. You don't *tell* me. You *ask* me and when I decline, you respect my wish to never see you again."

I chuckle at the idea. Who does she think she's dealing with? "Not in my world, Sunshine."

"Why did you call me that?"

"Because you're like a ray of fucking sunshine," I deadpan. "Now get your ass in the car."

"No."

"You're not a quick learner, are you?" I don't want to be rough with her, but she leaves me no choice. I get her into the car and Vincent closes the door. It locks as soon as he starts the engine.

"This is kidnapping! You can't do this!"

"Put your seat belt on."

"Jesus. What is wrong with you?"

I stop, turn to face her, drag the seat belt across her chest, and click it into place. "I don't like seeing some man put his hands on the woman I plan on fucking tonight."

Her mouth falls open.

"Please don't bullshit me, Emilia. You knew exactly—"

"Because you sent that note? You're insane."

"I know what I want."

"That doesn't mean you just take it. That's not how it works."

"It's how it works in my world, and guess what? You're in my world now, Sunshine."

"You can't just…just…"

I shake my head and look out the window as we approach my house. Vincent parks in the garage then discreetly goes inside. I open the door and climb out. She is already opening hers when I get to her side and immediately turns to walk over to the closing garage door, but she's not getting by me. I physically put my body between her and the exit. It's kind of funny when she starts twice, only to stop twice, like she thought for one moment that she could get past me.

"Inside," I say with a nod of my head

"No."

"You just don't fucking learn, do you?"

She opens her mouth to reply when I turn her and, keeping her arms behind her, I walk her up the stairs, to the door, and into the house. Once we're inside, I release her. She immediately goes to the counter, picks up an empty glass sitting there, and hurls it at me. I duck, and it crashes against the wall, shattering. I look at the mess, then at her and see that she's also looking at the floor, maybe just as surprised by her action as I am. More so, even.

When I take a step toward her, she takes one back, then turns and runs. I don't bother to run. I don't have to. I stalk after her through the kitchen and into the hallway to the locked front door, which she ridiculously tries to open again and again.

"Emilia." I watch as her spine goes rigid at the low command in my voice.

She turns, takes one look at me, and tries to slip past me

into the living room. I capture her arm, but she loses her balance. If I hadn't had her, she'd have gone sprawling.

I walk her backward until I have her by the wall, where I press her against it and cage her in with my hands on either side of her face.

"I think you like to be chased, don't you?"

"I hate you."

"Why? Because I make you lose your cool? Because I take away your control?"

"Fuck you."

"I plan to. I plan to fuck you every way humanly possible."

Her eyes go wide. She doesn't come back with a retort. I speak again.

"That includes this big mouth of yours." I lean in to kiss it, only to be met by a snapping of her teeth.

I smile, wipe my thumb over the spot, and see the smear of blood on my finger.

"You want it rough?" Her heart is racing, I see it in the maniacal throbbing of her pulse, in the quick rise and fall of her chest. "Because that's going to cost you."

"Let me go."

"Make me."

She narrows her eyes, exhales loudly, and shoves against my chest with both hands. I chuckle at her effort. She begins pounding her fists against me.

"Let me go!"

I lean in closer, so her face is distorted. "Make me," I repeat, my tone low, a threat, a warning, and a challenge all in one.

"Is this what you want? To fuck me? Will you let me go then?"

"Not likely."

But she keeps going like she hasn't heard me. "Because I don't think I can do the other thing." Her voice breaks, and her forehead creases. I'm thinking of a fuck, but her face is collapsing. All I can do is watch her. "I think..." She looks over my shoulder and shakes her head. There's a panic in her eyes when they finally meet mine. "I think you're going to hurt me."

She bites her lip, and tears glisten in her eyes. I get the feeling more and more that she's on the edge of something. Like she's standing on a precipice and her neatly controlled life—from the tight bun on her head, to the impeccable apartment, to her cool facade—it's all about to come toppling down.

And fuck me if I'm dealing with that shit when it happens. Because I know without a doubt she's gonna blow.

"I won't let him hurt you, if you're afraid of him."

"I'm not afraid of him!"

"Relax, Sunshine," I say, tapping her cheek lightly. "Take it easy."

"I'm not—"

"Just shut the fuck up and let me fuck you."

I press my mouth to hers and pull her hair out of that stupid bun because I need something to hold on to. A hundred pins drop to the floor, clinking delicately against the marble. I grip a handful of that lush mane and tilt her head back as I devour her mouth. Her hands are on my shoulders, and when I push her dress up to her waist and shove the crotch of her panties aside to finger her pussy, test how ready she is, she moans into my mouth.

I undo my belt, my jeans, and shove them down. I need to be inside her.

"I'm clean." I don't want to use a condom. I want to feel her. I need to. "You?"

She moans, nods her head, greedily reaches for my mouth. Holding her panties aside, I drive into her, making her gasp as her nails dig into my shoulders.

She's tight. Like really tight. And I'm watching her face, and I know I'm hurting her.

Her eyes come back into focus, and she squeezes her muscles around me. I pull out and thrust again. She makes a sound, a whimper, and my cock is harder for it, harder for that sound, her pain.

Pleasure and pain. She's confusing them. I see it in her eyes. I see it in the way she's biting her lip, drawing blood. I wonder if she's even aware of it, but I don't care.

I kiss her again, tasting that blood, fucking her harder. I feel her come, I hear that sound she made last night, and I impale her on my dick. The walls of her pussy are throbbing, and she's slick and hot as she comes on my dick, and fuck, I explode inside her, my mouth on hers, her clinging to me, fingernails digging into my neck, her cunt fucking milking me dry and still, I can't get enough.

5

EMILIA

My knees buckle when he sets me down. He catches me, but I shove his hands off. Force myself to stand on my own. One of my shoes has slipped off my foot. It's behind him. I balance on the other foot because he's already so freaking tall and big and I hate having to look up at him.

He only looks away for a moment to tuck his dick into his pants. I notice the little bit of pink on it. The smear of blood mixed with cum. He does too. I'm not a virgin, but it's been a long time since I've had sex, and he wasn't gentle. Even if he had been, though, he's big, and I'd probably bleed regardless. But I want it like this, anyway. I need him to hurt me, so I can come. It's sick, but I've always been like this. I'm sure some psychoanalyst would have a field day with it, but fuck that.

I adjust my panties and dress, but not before feeling his cum slide down my thighs. I press my legs together. I'd be mortified if he saw it, although he knows it's happening.

"Are you done? Can I go?" I don't even know why I ask. He won't let me go. I know that.

He cocks his head to the side. There is nothing casual in the way he looks at me. It's like he's studying me, constantly. Like he is really seeing me. Seeing inside of me. I just have to remember we're enemies. And I can't bury my head in the sand and hope he goes away. I know that's not how this is going to go. I can't roll over, give him what he wants. Because fucking me, it's just a bonus for him. He wants Alessandro, and I can't be there when he finds him. Which is a problem, because I'm the link. I'm the only one who can make him come out of whatever hole he's hiding in. But there will be a price. One I can't pay. I'm not ready for that.

He touches his thumb to my face. To the corner of my eye. He smears it across my cheek, and I realize it's a tear.

"What are you thinking?"

"That I don't like your cum sliding down my thighs."

He chuckles at that. "Bathroom's in there," he says, pointing down the hall. "Make it quick. I'll wash you properly later."

"I'd rather just go home and have a shower."

He steps back, snorts as he turns away, and walks into the living room. I watch him. He goes directly to the bar, and I know I'm not leaving, not just yet. I slide my foot into my sandal, and my heels click across the marble floor as I walk by the ornate staircase to the door beneath it.

The house is huge and quiet, so I assume it's just him and maybe that driver. Maybe more soldiers, who knows? It's pretty, too. Expensively done and from what I can see, extremely modern while maintaining the original design of the house. The bathroom is big and brightly lit with warm, flattering lighting. Marble from floor-to-ceiling, and the pedestal sink must be original, even though the fixtures are new. I run the tap and look at my reflection as I wash my hands. The soap smells good too. Sandalwood, I think. Like his aftershave.

"Dummy." I look away as I clean myself up.

I am a dummy. I am attracted to him. I want him. No, more than that. I just fucked a man I've known for two days. Without protection. A man who has told me he will hurt me if I don't deliver what he wants. And here I'm standing, thinking about how he looks. Thinking about how he looks at me.

I meet my reflection when I'm finished and brush out my hair with my fingers. I never wear it down, but I heard the pins fall to the floor when he pulled out my bun. Since I don't have my purse, I have nothing to secure the thick mass.

Most of the makeup I was wearing has worn off or been fucked off. I wipe the last trace of lipstick off the side of my mouth. When I'm done, I go back out to meet him.

I walk through the archway into the living room where I find Giovanni sitting on an armchair with a tumbler of whiskey in his hand. There's a second glass on the coffee table. He gestures to it. I take a moment to look around the space. Huge and dark, with charcoal, black, or stark white furnishings. Three large windows overlook the street, and while I can make out lights from passing cars it must be soundproofed because I can't hear any city noise. Sheer curtains provide some privacy, the heavier ones still secured to their holdbacks.

I walk inside and take a seat on the couch. I pick up the glass, sniff it.

"Do you have something else? I don't like whiskey."

"You drank it the other night, and you have a good collection of it."

"My father used to drink it. It's more of a memory, I guess."

He nods but doesn't make any rude comments. Instead he gets up and walks to the bar behind me.

"I'll take vodka if you have it," I say without turning around. I am looking at the paintings on the walls. They're also modern, and dark. Almost violent.

Ice clanks against crystal, and a moment later, I'm sipping vodka.

He resumes his seat. Resumes studying me.

"Did you eat dinner?"

I nod and concentrate on my glass. As uncomfortable as I feel, he seems to be the opposite.

I clear my throat. "We didn't use protection."

"You told me you were clean. I am too. I don't make it a habit to fuck without condoms. You?"

"None of your business."

"It became my business the moment I stuck my dick in you. But from how tight you are, I'm guessing it's been a while."

"Are you seriously saying that?"

"You bled."

"You didn't exactly give me time to adjust to your...size."

One corner of his mouth curves upward. "You came, Emilia. You liked it. You like my *size* and you like it rough."

I blink, unable to hold his gaze. He sees too much.

"What happened to you?"

I drink the last of my vodka, then swirl the ice around in the glass. He gets up and comes back with the bottle to refill my glass, then leaves the bottle on the coffee table before sitting back down, that same commanding air about him. Like he's the fucking king.

"Do you need to be hurt to come?"

I take a large swallow and refuse to look at him when I reply.

"Are we going to do a breakdown of the act? A moment-by moment-examination?" I ask, trying to keep my expression icy.

"Do those lines on your back have anything to do with it? Because those are something."

I don't answer. What can I say?

His expression is serious. "Who did it?"

I take the bottle and concentrate on pouring a third glass because the buzz I'd been working toward at the club is now gone.

"And more importantly, why?"

I look at him. "Did you bring me here to interrogate me?"

"No, I brought you here to fuck you."

I stand and fist my hands. "Well, since that's done, can I go now?"

"Not done," he says with a grin. "That was round one. Now sit down."

"I'm fine."

"Sit down."

I exhale loudly, then sit. Because it's kind of stupid to keep standing there.

We drink our drinks, him watching me, me feeling the burn of his eyes on me. "Who whipped you, Emilia?"

I flinch at the word. Whipped. Like it's the Dark fucking Ages.

"Why do you care?" I ask, swallowing more vodka.

"I'm curious, that's all. It's in my nature."

"You said you'd hurt me if I don't find Alessandro," I say, wanting to change the subject.

"I said I don't want to hurt you."

"But that doesn't mean you won't."

He leans his head back, his eyes slanting as they devour

me. The longer we sit like this, the more anxious I feel. I pour my fourth vodka.

"Slow down on that."

I shrug a shoulder.

"When was the last time you saw him?"

"A month after my father was murdered." My voice breaks. I hope he thinks it's because of the painful memory of the attack on my father.

"You were close with him? Your father?"

I nod.

"And it's just the two of you, you and Alessandro now?"

"Yes." I imagine he's done his homework and knows my mother died in childbirth.

"Were you daddy's princess?"

I hope he can read the hate in my glare. I think he can. "My father was a good man. He was a fair man. An honest one."

At that, he laughs outright. "He was a cartel boss. I'm pretty sure he was none of those things, however much you like to deceive yourself."

"You don't know anything about him. Don't judge him by how you are."

"I'm not denying who I am. I don't hide from what I do. I mean, you're the one who lives in the lap of luxury and pretends you do it off the money you earn managing events at a hotel. The one who went so far as to change her name to get away from her past, yet isn't too good to use the blood money earned from the exact thing she's running from. At least I don't run from who I am."

"You don't know anything about me. I paid for everything. I paid for every fucking thing."

"With the skin of your back, you mean?"

I feel hot tears sting my eyes. He's not going to stop until he finds out. He won't stop until he knows.

"Did I hit the nail on the head? Huh? Is that it, *Em*?"

Rage burns inside me, starting at my core, spreading through my veins, pumping adrenaline through my body. I'm on my feet before I know it, and that smirk, that fucking smirk, is back on his face. I hate him. I hate him and his intrusion into my life. It's taken me so fucking long to get here. So long to be this okay, and he's just going to stroll in and blow it all to hell. And what's worse is I'm letting him. I'm so fucking weak. So fucking damaged that I can't do anything but fucking cry.

I fist my hands at my sides. He must see something inside my eyes because he rises too.

"You think you can hurt me? Damage me, somehow? You think you can break me as you sit there and judge me and push me and push me until I tell you what you think you want to know?"

"Sit down." He's not smiling anymore as he takes a step toward me.

"And for what? What fucking business is it of yours? What you have with my brother, whatever that is, it has nothing to do with me. He owes you something? Take it out of his fucking skin. Not mine."

"Be careful."

I look at him, then around the room. I don't know what I'm looking for. Something to throw? Something to hurt him with? I know how that ended last time. But I do have one weapon because I've done my homework too.

I step toward him, poke my finger into his chest. "You think you can sit back and judge me, judge my father, from your high horse, when all you are is a liar. A betrayer." I feel how strange my smile must look. How unnatural. "I can find things out too, you know. Things about you. Why isn't there a single family photo in your house, Giovanni? Why not one single fucking picture?"

"I'm warning you."

But I go on because I can't stop. I don't even want to. It's like I want to push him.

"I know why. You want me to tell you? You want me to tell you how much I know about you?"

He takes my wrist, twists it. It hurts, but I can't let that stop me.

"Please do."

"I know you put your father in a wheelchair. I know you pay to have him looked after. Have been for years. I guess you're not a good shot if you didn't kill him, huh? I know why, too," I say as he walks me backward until I feel something hard at my back—the dining-room table. I know from the look on his face that I should stop. That I should shut up now. But I don't. I don't want to. "He fucked your girlfriend, didn't he?"

The change in him is instantaneous.

He whirls me around, pushes me down over the table, and is shoving the skirt of my dress up to my waist and, as sick as it is, I want it.

So I keep pushing.

Because I'm nothing if not self-destructive. I'm like a time bomb waiting to go off. Have been for a long time. I wonder how I've kept it together for so long, actually.

He leans over me, and I feel him, his hardness, the only barrier between us the thin material of my panties and his pants.

"She was my tutor, actually," he whispers, his hands in the waistband of my panties, pushing them down and off one foot as he kicks my legs apart. "Not my girlfriend. I was fifteen when I first fucked her." I hear him undoing his jeans, and it takes all I have not to arch my back. To push back into him because I need this. I need this so fucking bad. And when he thrusts into my wet passage, I suck in a loud breath and scratch my fingernails into the polished wood of the table.

"And no, I didn't want to kill him. I wanted him in that fucking chair." He lays down over my back, licks the side of my face. His breathing is ragged too, his face wet with sweat. "And you know what else? You look just like her."

I stop at that, process his slowly, purposefully spoken words. It's hard, though, hard to think. But one glance at him tells me he's processing too. Like he hadn't intended to say that. But then he talks, and he's just an asshole.

"But if you wanted to know, all you had to do was ask," he whispers at my ear as he pulls out of me, draws back. When I try to straighten, he shoves me back down and takes both my wrists into his one hand, holding them at my lower back.

"You want it, don't you?" he asks, slapping my ass. "Admit it."

"No."

"Look at me."

"Fuck you."

He slaps my ass again, three sharp spanks on my right cheek. "Look at me," he repeats.

I do and I'm gritting my teeth. When I meet his eyes, he smiles wide and just as he does, he pushes his finger first into my pussy, then slides it up to my asshole.

"You want it." It's not a question. He sinks his finger into the tight passage, and it hurts, but fuck, it feels good too and he knows it. He can see it on my face.

"You think you can wound me with this pathetic crumb

of information?" he asks as his thick cock stretches my pussy, sliding in once, twice before he pulls out, and I feel him trailing it up to my asshole. "Let me teach you about hurt." And he pushes the head of his cock inside me without warning, making me cry out.

It fucking burns, and I can't breathe for a minute. I'm fisting my hands, digging my nails into my own palms.

"How's that for hurt, *Em*?" He pushes a little deeper. I whimper, and I hate myself for it. "You have a tight ass. You gonna be able to take all of me?" He pushes again.

"Please."

"What's that?"

"Please. It hurts."

He leans down over me again. "I'm only about a third of the way in, Sunshine. You've got a long way to go. I'd try to relax if I were you." He claims another inch, and a sound comes from inside my throat, a wail or sob. A wound.

"I'm sorry," I cry out.

"No, you're not." He pulls out a little, affording me the smallest relief, the rest almost momentary because when he pushes in again, he takes more of me. "Not yet, at least."

I gasp, my eyes bulging at the next inch.

"But remember how I told you I didn't want to hurt you?" he asks, and I feel one hand snake around, fingers finding my clit. "Do you, Emilia?"

He's rubbing my clit, and I know this sensation. Pain and pleasure. I mix them up, he's mixing them up, and I'm arching back against him.

"Do you?"

I nod my head. This feels good. I don't want him to stop.

"That's it, relax. Good girl." He draws out a little, pumping in and out, small movements as he claims more of me, and it hurts but it feels good, too, and I'm going to come soon. I squeeze my eyes shut, and I hear him behind me, hear him give me his permission—that bastard—and I obey. I come with his dick in my ass and his fingers rubbing my clit, and when I do, he pushes all the way inside me and it's like I'm tumbling from orgasm to orgasm. My knees give out; I can't stand on my own. I can hardly breathe, and that noise, that animal like wail, it's me. It's coming from me because he's fucking me now, fucking me hard and deep, and when I hear him come, feel his release, feel him fill me up, I can't hold on anymore. I can't breathe. I can't speak. I can't beg him to stop. Beg him to never stop. Stars dance before my eyes. I lay my head down, and all I can do is feel. Feel him inside me. Feel him possess me. Hurt me. Own me. Feel myself being owned by him.

I must pass out because when I open my eyes again, I'm in his powerful arms and my head is bouncing against his chest. He's carrying me up the stairs. I look up at him. His face is stern, serious, and he doesn't look at me as he takes me up yet another flight. I let my eyes close. I don't open them again, even when I feel him lay me on a bed.

It smells like him. I'm in his bed and he's taking off my dress and I just lie there and let him. I'm going in and out of sleep, but it's not just sleep, the pull is more powerful than that. He's gone one minute but back the next. He's cleaning me and the water is warm and he's gentle.

I protest, I try to, but he tells me to shush. When he's done, he pulls the blankets up over me and leans down close to my ear. I don't know if he thinks I can hear him or not when he says what he says. It's the smallest whisper. But I do hear it. And I wish I didn't.

"To answer your question, no, I don't think I can break you, Emilia. I think you're already broken."

6

GIOVANNI

She's sleeping so deeply, she barely stirs when, two hours later, I climb into bed. She's lying on her side with her back to me. I push the blanket down to her waist. I look at her back, I study it, feel the texture of scar tissue beneath my fingers. Count the lines. Twenty-one. Her back was nearly opened. It was in some places. It speaks of violence and hate, and it's strange to see it on her. On her skin. She must take pains to hide it. And the strange, sick thing is, I find it beautiful. I find her more beautiful for it. Stronger. Even if I do want to kill the bastard who did it.

I think about her taking it. I wonder if she offered herself for it or had to be held down. Maybe she was knocked out beforehand. A mercy. But no, I don't think so. What would be the point? This was a lesson or maybe a warning. Or both. Something she could hide but would never forget.

Whatever it was, it's part of her now.

And what I said about her already being broken, this is part of that breaking.

She's afraid of her brother. I want to know why. I get the

feeling she's more afraid of him than of me. That makes me even more curious, and I have a feeling the scars on her back have something to do with that fear. I want to know about their relationship. I want to know about her father's murder. That was four years ago. She claims not to have seen Alessandro in that long, and I believe her. I can find him on my own, but it'll take longer. I have a feeling when she contacts him, he'll come. And as much as she doesn't want that, I want the opposite. Because I want to see them together with my own eyes. I won't let him hurt her. I won't let him lay a finger on her. But I do need them in a room together.

I wrap my arm around her middle and pull her into me. I told her she reminded me Angelica. It's not that, though. She's nothing like Angelica. Angelica gave the illusion of being naive, but she was selfish. Manipulative even, at least until the end. Emilia is not those things. She is simply broken. But having her in my arms, it's bringing up old memories. Stirring the dust of the past. I have to remember this, remember to keep them separate.

Emilia mumbles something and turns, but her eyes are still closed and she's still asleep, even as she burrows into me, tucking her arms between us and her head into the crook of my arm. I lie still watching her, and I wonder what the fuck I'm doing.

As well as she sleeps that night, I don't. Just when I nod off, my phone vibrates on the nightstand. I roll onto my back to check the screen. It's Hugo Drake, Killian Black's man. And he's got one of Alessandro Estrella's boys.

I glance at Emilia, who is on her back, her face turned slightly toward me and more relaxed than I've ever seen her. She's so soft when she's like this. So different than when she's awake and so tightly wound. Her cheeks are flushed and her long lashes sweep downward, so long they almost cast a shadow all their own. Her lips are swollen and slightly parted. I need to stop looking at them because I'm going to want to do things if I don't and this is important. I quietly get out of bed and, so as not to wake her, use the shower in one of the guest rooms. Before heading out, I leave instructions she's not to leave the house until I return.

I make a call to have several of my men meet me at Mea Culpa, and when I arrive, I use the side entrance where I'm obviously expected. The cook's already making breakfast, and the smell of frying bacon makes me hungry.

"Morning, Mr. Santa Maria," someone says once I'm inside. He's a low-level soldier.

"Morning."

"They're waiting for you downstairs. Last door on the right."

"Thanks." I'm about to head down but stop. "Get me some coffee, will you?"

"Sure thing, Mr. Santa Maria."

The downstairs of Mea Culpa is infamous in our world. It's where you absolutely do not want to be because nothing good happens there. This is where the ugly side of this business is handled. Upstairs is high-end, with an excellent restaurant and only the most beautiful women to provide service and entertainment. Down here, it's a whole other world, and you know it the moment you step through the door that leads to the metal staircase.

It's cold with bright fluorescent lighting and is lined with heavy doors. The one I'm directed to has two men standing outside. They nod in greeting as one opens the door. Hugo chose a good room for today's purposes. He knows me. It's tiled with a drain in the middle and a counter along one end, like a kitchen, but not. Just has all the tools one may require.

"Good morning, sir." A soldier straightens, greets me upon entering.

I nod, and he resumes picking dirt out from under his fingernails as I turn to Hugo, who is leaning against the wall at the back.

"Morning," I say.

"Good morning."

He's a big guy and looks foreboding with his heavily tattooed arms folded across his chest. He's wearing a black T-shirt, black jeans, and dark shoes. He's ready for the work that needs to be done.

I turn my attention at the man sitting on a metal folding chair in the middle of the room, wrists bound behind his back, looking up at me like a wounded animal. Like he knows what's coming because I know for a fact he's been in this situation before, just on the other end of things. He knows what happens to the guy in the chair.

"Good Morning," I say to him.

When he doesn't reply, Hugo swiftly stalks up behind the chair, grips a handful of his hair and tugs his head backward. "Mr. Santa Maria just bid you good morning. Show some fucking respect."

"G...g..."

"This is one of Estrella's men?" I guess I didn't expect him to be so easily broken down.

"John Diaz. And I admit, he looked a little better before the trip over here," Hugo says, one side of his mouth curving upward. He takes pleasure from this.

I look at the cheap, bloodied suit, at the man's bruised face. His pleading eyes.

"It happens. Where'd you find him?" I reach into the

front pocket of the guy's jacket, pull out the piece of paper sticking out. It's an address. I don't know the area, but it's a little outside the city. I tuck the piece of paper into my pocket.

"All-night diner near his house."

"I don't do work for Mr. Estrella anymore," the man in the chair says.

"That's about all he's been telling us too," Hugo says, picking a piece of skin off his knuckle. "Except I know he was on a job when we picked him up."

I look down at the man again, peer into his face. "You high, Johnny?"

Hugo snorts.

"No. No, sir."

"I think we beat the high out of him because he was behaving like a fool, weren't you, Johnny-boy?"

The man in the chair flinches.

"What job?"

Hugo gestures to the pocket in which I just stuck the piece of paper. "Has to do with that address, but that's all I got, so far. Was waiting on you, thinking you may want to talk to him while he still has the ability to speak."

The man blubbers something.

"So you don't work for Estrella, but you were doing a job for him?"

"I owed him a favor. This is it. I'm out. I can't—" He shakes his head, drops it.

"Can't what?"

He doesn't answer right away. I turn to Hugo. "Pet peeve of mine. I can't stand it when people don't finish their fucking sentences."

"I hear you." Hugo kicks the leg of Diaz's chair, and he startles.

"Can't what?" I repeat.

"I got a family now. Please. I don't want nothing to do with Estrella."

"Considering that, I hope I wasn't out of line to offer a deal," Hugo says, moving around so the man can see his face. "I guess it's my soft side."

I chuckle because Hugo doesn't have a soft side. None of us do. He's fucking with the guy, but I'll play along.

"What's the deal?" This guy's about pissing himself right now, and I'm good with that.

"He gives us the information we require, and we let him live. Of course, he promises never to speak again. Can't take a chance he'll share that information with anyone else, obviously. Just covering all our bases."

"You're thorough. But you weren't authorized to make that deal, were you?" I turn to the man. "He doesn't make the decisions. I think you've been misled."

"No. Please, please, sir. Mr. Santa Maria. Please. Estrella, he's ruthless."

I raise an eyebrow. "That's funny." I pick up a folding chair that's leaning against the far wall, bring it over in front of the guy, open it, and sit. "But I don't think it's Estrella you need to worry about right now. You mentioned you had family?" I use the past tense on purpose, and I see from the change in expression on his face he catches it.

He nods. "A wife and a boy."

"How old is the boy?"

"Two."

"Great age, isn't it? So innocent."

He nods again, and I see a glimpse of hope on his face.

"He won't have much memory of you."

That hope is gone almost as quickly as it came. His eyes grow huge, and they're filling up with tears.

I shake my head. "Crying is for women. Don't be a fucking pussy. You lived this life, you know how it works. I'm damn sure your hands aren't clean."

He can't seem to stop himself, though.

"Estrella, where is he?"

"I don't know. I really don't. I haven't done work for him since Mr. Em—" he stops, catches himself.

"Since?" I raise my eyebrows. "Tell me, and I'll see what I can do about keeping the deal Hugo made with you."

He considers this. I get up and move the chair away because the smell of his fear is making me nauseous.

"I don't know where he is. I swear it."

"Since his what, Johnny?"

"He'll kill me. My family."

"No, I'll be the one to kill you, which will then leave your family unprotected. Alessandro Estrella is one mean son of a bitch, but I'll let you in on a secret. I'm meaner. Hugo, give him some incentive."

I've barely finished my sentence before Hugo's behind him. A moment later, the chair goes crashing forward and I hear the collision of the man's face against the tiles.

"Ouch," I say, watching as Hugo straightens the chair. There's a wide gash across his forehead and he looks to have lost at least one tooth.

Hugo then grips his hair and tugs his head backward.

"Your wife, does she know where you are?"

He tries to shake his head no.

"You don't want her or that kid of yours in here, do you?"

"No. Please, Mr. Santa Maria."

"Let him go, Hugo."

Hugo reluctantly releases his hair.

"Now talk. Last chance." I check my watch.

"Mr. Estrella. Emil Estrella. It's the last job I did for Alessandro."

I study him. I know he's not lying to me, and he's actually confirming something I've suspected all along. Emil Estrella's death was an inside job.

"You were responsible for Emil Estrella's assassination?"

"Alessandro was very angry at his father."

"And his sister? Emilia? Was he also very angry at her?" The words are out before I can stop them.

The man goes dead still at the mention of her name, and his eyes are about to bulge out of his head. A moment later, he hangs his head down, and I can see he's crying again.

The door opens then. The man I'd asked to get me a cup of coffee apologizes for interrupting and hands me a steaming cup.

"Thank you. I'm fucking starving. Hugo, you have breakfast yet?"

"Not yet. Up too early with this fool."

"Let's wrap this up and get some food. I swear I can still smell the bacon frying up there."

Hugo chuckles. "It's damn good bacon."

I give him a nod and take a sip of my coffee.

Hugo grips the man's hair again and tugs his head backward. "Where the fuck is Estrella?"

"I swear I don't know. Someone called in the job. I don't even know who it was. I swear I would tell you if I knew. I swear on my family. I swear on my kid."

Hugo releases him, steps backward.

"What's the address on that piece of paper?" I ask, sipping my coffee.

He shakes his head, looks like a broken man.

"You want to tell me, I know you do. I can see it."

Nothing.

"Help me to help you, Johnny. But I have to be honest here, even if I could honor Hugo's deal, how would we make sure you don't speak again?" I cock my head to the side and wait for him to catch on because there's no getting around this. He'll be punished, and his punishment will serve as a warning for anyone harboring Alessandro Estrella. I want Estrella to know I'm coming for him. Dominic Benedetti may be the one to pull the trigger, but he made his deal with me. He made me look like a fool when he ran out on it, and I will deliver him to my cousin alive, but that doesn't mean I won't punish him first. "Dead men are the only ones I know who don't talk."

"Men without tongues don't talk either," Hugo adds, typing something into his phone and tucking it into his pocket before moving to look through the drawers for something. I can guess what.

The man in the chair goes gray and literally pisses himself. I step back. "Christ, these are expensive clothes."

"Please. Please!" Johnny begs as Hugo comes over with a steak knife.

"Your life in exchange for your tongue."

The man is struggling against his bonds, and sobbing like a fucking pussy.

"Think of your family. Think how happy they'll be to have you back. It's just your tongue, after all."

"Please."

"Think about the boy. Look, we'll even use a sharp knife. It'll slice right through the meaty flesh."

He whimpers, sobs, pleads.

I nod at the other soldier who's been quiet. "I want to know what's at this address. If he tells you before I find out myself, he lives, minus his tongue. If he doesn't talk, cut off his tongue anyway then kill the bastard."

"Yes, sir."

I turn to the man in the chair. "You understand the importance of timing here, Johnny? It's going to take me maybe an hour to get out to that address. You think about that."

He mumbles something, but I turn to Hugo.

"Ready for breakfast?"

"Fuck, yeah." He hands the knife off to the soldier who eagerly takes it.

"Let's go."

When I reach the door, I turn back to the soldier still inside. "Make sure if he does choose the first option, he doesn't bleed out. That'd make a liar out of me."

Hugo and I walk out the door, and the screaming stops the instant it closes behind us. I reach into my pocket and hand the address over to Vincent. "Get some men to this address. I want to know who's out there."

After breakfast, I head into one of the upstairs rooms for a meeting, where I'm tied up for most of the day. What I really want to do, though, is go back home. To see her. But Vincent hands me an envelope as soon as I get into the car.

"What is it?"

"Letter couriered to the girl's house. Our man intercepted it."

I open the rather bulky envelope and reach inside to retrieve another, smaller one. This one is good quality stationary, heavy, and specially made. I already recognize it. My blood boils.

I turn it over. It's addressed to Emilia Larrea-Estrella. I guess he's covering all his bases. That bulk I felt, it's the wax seal. Fucking pompous, arrogant fool thinks he's some kind of aristocracy with his fucking seal. I rip the envelope open.

Dearest Emilia,

Ghosts we think we killed and buried always lurk nearby, ready to snatch us back in time. Ready to smother us in darkness.

Do not trust my son. He will hurt you like he hurt her.

Be safe.

Your friend,

A.

I crumple the note but decide not to throw it away. I tuck it into my pocket instead.

"How in fuck's name does he know about her?" I ask Vincent, although I know it's a redundant question.

"I don't know, sir," he answers anyway. I know I have enemies, and many of them are his spies. He lives for vengeance, my father.

"I'm going to fucking kill him. Let's go."

"The Lincoln property?"

I nod once. The Lincoln property is a large and completely private estate on the outskirts of the city. It's currently occupied by my father, and I wonder as I fume if I can't throw the old man out on the street. Wonder what the hell debt I owe the bastard.

We pull through the gates a little over an hour later. The property is so large, you can't see the house itself for another few minutes and, after that, it's still a mile to the front doors. With thirteen bedrooms, it's bigger than my house in the city, but he's still not satisfied. He wants more. Greedier and greedier in his old age.

No one stops me when I walk in the front door, although the woman dusting is startled at my entrance.

"Where's my father?" I ask her. I don't know her name,

and she's quite young. She most likely doesn't know who I am.

I ask my question again, louder this time.

Footsteps upstairs tell me someone's heard, and when I look up, I see Janet, my father's nurse. She's been in my employ ever since the accident. Or what she calls the accident. My father and I both know it was not that.

"Giovanni? Is that you?"

She comes down the stairs. She's in her early fifties and the only one who can stand to be around my father. Staff turnover is at an astonishing rate here because he's such a dick. She reaches the landing and comes to greet me. I can barely spare a smile. I'm too angry. "Where is he?"

"He just went to bed to lie down for a bit." Her expression changes. She is his nurse, after all. She may not know the reasons for our shared hatred of each other, but she knows the depth of it.

"I want to talk to him."

"Come have a cup of coffee." She takes my arm, tries to lead me toward the kitchen.

"I'm not here for coffee."

Her expression tells me she has some idea why I'm here. "Gio—"

"Now, Janet. Take me to him."

"He needs his rest. He's an old man. Why don't you two work out whatever differences you have? The past is dead, and he will be too, soon. You'll regret it, Giovanni."

I snort. "I won't regret his death, Janet."

With that, I walk past her and up the stairs. She follows, but I'm much faster and, a few minutes later, I'm standing inside the master bedroom, a grand room fit for a king but occupied by this peasant.

My father must have been expecting me because he's

sitting up in his large, four-poster bed, the blanket over his legs, a cigar between his fingers, a wicked grin on his rotting face.

"Ah, the prodigal son returns."

"I'd be more respectful, old man." The curtains are drawn and the room is dark, the air rank.

"What brings you to visit your dying father?"

Hands fisted, I step deeper into the room, stop a few feet from the bed. "If only I could be so lucky." I take the crumpled note from my pocket, read it out loud. "What the hell is this?"

"Just want to be sure the girl is on her guard. Her safety is my only concern."

"The girl is none of your business."

"Pretty thing, I hear. With a striking resemblance to—"

"You stay away from her. Any of your spies come near her, and I'll kill them, understand?"

He grins. "Did I hit a nerve?" He leans over to stub the cigar out in the ashtray on the nightstand.

He did. Fuck. I ball up the note and toss it on the bed. "Stay out of my life. Stay out of my business, or I will cut you off."

"You're a sorry son of a bitch, you know that?"

"You can say what you want about me, but don't you dare talk about my mother that way."

"It's a fucking expression."

I walk around the bed and when I lean in, he leans away. He's scared of me, but his hatred is much more powerful than his fear.

"Hear me, father. Hear me well. The only reason you're alive is because of my siblings. I don't want to hurt them anymore than they've already been hurt. But you fuck with me, and I will fuck with you back, understand?"

"Threatening an old, helpless man. You make me sick, boy."

I fist my hands.

"Giovanni!" It's Janet, standing at the door.

I take my father by the collar and draw him forward. "Do you understand?"

"That's enough!" Janet suddenly has my arm and is trying to drag me off him.

My father's watery eyes still have that same hardness in them, that hatred. I wonder if he always hated me or if it was only after Angelica.

I release him and step back.

Janet moves around me and adjusts the collar of his pajamas.

"I'm fine," I hear him tell her when I reach the door. "You should bring her here," he calls out as I step into the hallway. I stop. "I'd love to have a look at her with my own eyes."

My hands fist again. Janet comes rushing out, closing the bedroom door behind her.

I turn to her. "I don't want any more letters. No contact. You know the agreement."

"I'll keep an eye on him. He's just an old man."

"Don't underestimate him, Janet."

She just gives me a shake of her head. I walk out of the house, glad to be outside, glad to breathe in fresh air after that suffocating room.

I will never bring Emilia here. I will never let him see her. Touch her. Never. I'll fucking kill him before I allow that.

In a few minutes, I'm in the car and heading home. Maybe what I'm doing is a mistake. When I went to Emilia's apartment, it was about her brother. Now though, it's different. It's more than that. Hell, I'm fucking her. And I can't get enough of it. Of her.

I'm not fool enough to believe I've scared my father off, though. He has nothing but hate. Hate and time.

And I have to be careful with her. I can't ever allow him anywhere near Emilia.

7
EMILIA

"*I don't think I can break you, Emilia. I think you're already broken.*"

I'm glad it's Saturday, and I don't have to see Katy just yet after last night. I'm sure she's spread the news of my being carried out of that club caveman-style over Giovanni's shoulder. Although at this point, does it matter? With Giovanni hell-bent on finding Alessandro, on using me to lure him, I'm going to have to disappear anyway.

Giovanni is closer to the truth than he realizes.

His was right when he guessed I paid with my skin. But it wasn't just the brutal physical reminder Alessandro left me with. There was more. Hell, by the time we got to that part, to him opening me up like that, I was already broken beyond repair. The whipping was pure rage. Pure, violent hate.

Tears sting my eyes, and I wipe them with the heel of my hand. I'm sitting in the garden behind Giovanni's house, watching the moon and forcing down whiskey. When I woke today, I got dressed in the dress I'd worn last night and made my way downstairs, grateful not to run into anyone as

I searched for my panties and shoes, which were on the dining-room floor. I'd just slipped into my shoes when a woman came into the room and asked what I wanted for breakfast. I told her I'd be leaving but thanked her and had been informed that Mr. Santa Maria wanted me looked after until he got home that evening. I almost argued with her, but then one of his men turned up behind her—I think he'd been at my apartment too. He dismissed her and told me I would be not be permitted to leave the property. From the tone of his voice, there was no discussion to be had. He told me if I needed anything to ask him, and he would take care of it.

And now it's past nine at night and Giovanni's still not here and I'm in his garden, drinking his best whiskey. It burns, and I feel like I want to vomit with every swallow but if I drink enough of it, I can forget that part and remember when I was little and how my father and I would sit in his study and how I was safe. Protected. I remember how powerful he was. Like a king. No, like a god. One word from him and every fear was banished, every enemy slayed. Even Alessandro.

And I know it's one of the reasons Alessandro hates me.

When we were younger, I taunted Alessandro with my father's love. That's another thing Giovanni's right about. I was daddy's princess. Even when we were little, from my earliest memories, my brother was as hated as I was loved. In my father's eyes, he was to blame for our mother's death.

I didn't understand then what I was doing. I didn't understand that Alessandro's hatred of my father encompassed his whole world, including me. Everything and everyone our father loved, he hated, he would hurt. Even Mel, our ancient dog, my father's constant companion, he poisoned.

I wonder if I had been kinder to him if things might have been different. I wonder if I'd pled his case to my father, told him it wasn't his fault mom died, that it didn't make any sense, that it was as much my fault as Alessandro's—because she died in childbirth—that things would be different today.

It's too late for that, though.

My mother was a petite woman and carrying us in her belly had taken its toll on her. Twins would have been hard enough, but we weren't twins. There were three of us at first. One of my brothers died when my mother was not quite seven months pregnant, which is why they'd needed to operate, to get us out. To get him out.

But during the surgery, she lost too much blood, and she was already so weak, and she died just as they took Alessandro from her belly.

That's why dad blamed him. And the fact that he looked so much like her, that every time he saw him, he saw what he'd lost. If I look at photographs of her, I can see how people would say he is her spitting image. But to me, the features on her were soft. Warm and full of love. On him, they're hard. Cold and cruel. Like his heart.

But how much of that is my fault? I am guilty for never having protected him. For wanting to be daddy's princess. For wanting to be the one he loved most.

Don't I deserve what I got?

The moon keeps disappearing behind the clouds. I feel light drops of rain, but they're gone as soon as they start. The relief from the heat is temporary.

I pour more of the whiskey and get up to walk around the walled-in space. I don't even hear the sounds of the city here. The garden is nestled in a way that you almost wouldn't know you were in a city. It's strange. I'm so used to that noise. I'm going to miss it when I leave. And I do have to leave.

Unless I have Giovanni's protection.

No, that's not an option. Protection from him would come at a price. I can't pay that. I only have one option.

I dip my toe in the pool and watch the surface ripple. I'm tempted to strip off my clothes and let myself slip in, float there. Slip beneath the surface.

But I'm too much of a coward for that.

I think about what he said about his tutor. That I look like her. What does that even mean? Is that why he wants me? I remind him of his first love?

With each passing minute, I'm growing angrier and angrier at myself, at my imprisonment. I looked around his bedroom today. Snooped a little. I figured it was my right. But I didn't find anything out of the ordinary apart from a stash of cash. I guess a man in his line of work will always have cash like that lying around. I didn't have much privacy to go through the other rooms, but I should have tried harder. I'm too obedient.

I go back to my seat and lay back and watch the sky, watch the clouds move across it, watch the big trees. It's so pretty here, different than my rooftop, but I like it.

When I finally hear his voice, it's close to nine-thirty. I turn my head to look at him. He opens one of the French doors and walks outside. He's taken off his suit jacket and is rolling up his shirt sleeves. His eyes are all dark and intense, and they trap me the instant he sets them on me. I can't look away if I try. His dark hair is ruffled, and he has that constant shadow along his jaw, that scruff that I still remember when he surprised me in my bed that first night.

I feel my face heat up at that memory and the one of last night. Of when I came so hard that I passed out.

He stops when he's a few feet from me, eyes the bottle. I make a point of giving him a smirk as I finish my glass of his expensive whiskey.

"I thought you didn't like that stuff?" he says, coming around to take the glass from me. He looks distracted. On edge. He pours for himself in the same glass and drinks while standing there, looming over me. "Why aren't you wearing the clothes I had delivered?"

"Because I have my own clothes."

"I thought you'd be more comfortable."

"If you're worried about my comfort, then you should let me go home."

He looks over the length of me, and his gaze falls at my bare feet. I think how vulnerable I am. How much at his mercy. I swing my legs off and make to stand, but I must be light-headed because I stumble. He has to catch me so I don't fall.

"Steady."

My hands are against his chest. A moment later, I shove against him. "Let me go."

He does, and I take a step back and wonder where I left my shoes because without my heels, I'm so much smaller than him. I look at his hand as he brings the glass to his mouth. To the dusting of hair on his arm, the expensive watch. I watch him drink, swallow. I remember what he did to me last night. I remember his hands on me. Remember him inside me and again, I feel my face and my core heat up.

When I meet his eyes, he's watching me. "How much did you drink?"

I shrug a shoulder. "Don't worry about me. I can hold my liquor."

"Did you swim at least?"

"I'm not on vacation," I say. "I was told this morning I

wouldn't be permitted to leave the house, in fact, which makes me a prisoner. What is this, house arrest? Is this what you have to resort to to keep a woman?"

He grins and walks over to the pool. "Nah. You're just special."

"I want to go home. I demand it."

He chuckles, sets down his glass, and starts to strip off his clothes.

"What are you doing?"

He's got his shoes and socks off, is undoing the buttons of his shirt, and a moment later, it's off. Then his slacks. He turns to me.

"Swimming. Let's go. In."

"No. I told you, I'm not swimming."

"It'll cool you down, and trust me, you need to cool down because your attitude's going to get you into trouble. You don't want a repeat of last night—or do you? I imagine your ass is probably sore."

I glare, but he just gives me a smirk before pushing his briefs down and off and diving into the pool. He doesn't resurface until he's gone the length of it, and when he does, he gracefully changes direction and swims a lap to the opposite end. All I can do is watch because he's beautiful. He's so fucking beautiful. His body is a perfect harmony of muscle, power, and speed. He glides through the water, effortlessly going back and forth and back and forth, seeming tireless. As if he doesn't have a care in the world. When he does finally stop, he catches my eye. I can't look away as he draws himself out of the water, his muscles bulging, his hair and body dripping, glistening.

He stands there and lets me look at him, and I do. I'm speechless.

He is your enemy.

He is your enemy.

But my brain can't seem to make any sense to the rest of me because I'm staring like a fool.

"Come here."

I clear my throat and shake my head.

All it takes are two steps from him and he's got his arms around me. He's wet and cold. The next thing I know, he's lifting me off the ground, and I scream when he tosses me into the pool.

Panic sets in instantly. I open my eyes. Bubbles are all around me, and that cloudy, echo-like sound drenches my ears, fills me with terror. I think I'm screaming, but then, an instant before I need to breathe, his strong arms are around me and he's lifting me up. I break the surface.

"You can't fucking swim?"

I'm clinging to him and sputtering water and I want to cry and scream all at once. He's got me pressed between the edge of the pool and himself, and all I feel beneath my feet is water. He mutters another curse, this one to himself.

"You really don't know how to swim?" he asks a little more gently.

I shake my head, and the coughing finally ceases. I'm embarrassed. "I want to get out."

"You're fine."

"No. I want out."

"I've got you. You're safe."

I look up at him, and I don't know if it's his words or the way he's looking at me or the whiskey or fuck, I don't know what it is, but I start to sob. I'm clinging to him and pushing him away all at once and he's just letting me, he's letting me and holding me and keeping me up and fuck. I'm losing it. He's going to make me lose it.

"Let me go!"

"No."

"Please!"

"No. I won't let you go."

I look at him. He's watching me and next thing I know, he's got his hands under my arms and he's lifting me out. He sets me at the edge of the pool and, with his arms on either side of me, he lifts himself out. He kisses me and pushes me backward as he lays his weight on me.

I should fight.

I should want to fight, to hit him, to pound against him as little good as it will do, but I don't want to. I just want to lay here beneath him, and I want to feel him kiss me. Feel him watch me, feel him want me.

He pulls back, looks down at me. His eyes are dark, the pupils dilated. He nudges my legs apart and then he's between them and my dress is hiked up to my waist. I feel him at my entrance, feel his thick cock. I reach up to pull him to me, but with his hands on either side of my face, he halts me. I close my eyes when I feel him begin to penetrate, but he stops that too.

"Open your eyes, Emilia."

I blink them open, and I feel the heat of tears again.

"I want to watch you."

He kisses me. I taste chlorine and him and I watch him, too, as he enters me. It's different this time. It's slower, and I can feel every inch of him. I'm clinging to him, and it's like I can't get close enough, like I can't get warm enough, like I can't have enough of him to hide me, to keep me locked beneath him and hidden from view. I'm crying again and fuck, this is going to kill me. This slow fucking, this love-making, it's going to destroy me.

"You are so fucking beautiful when you cry."

A moment later, I feel the tip of his tongue catch a tear

and trace it upward. I hear a strange sound like a sob or something desperate, and I just need him to fuck me. To fuck me hard and make me come. He knows it, and he's not giving it to me.

"You want to break me."

He shakes his head. "I told you last night. You're already broken."

He did tell me. He did. I dig my nails into his back, and I know it hurts him when I feel his skin give, when I know I'm drawing blood, but he won't move faster, and he won't let me go, he won't even let me look away. But then he moves one hand to cradle the back of my head, but that cradling is only momentary before his hand turns into a fist in my hair and he squeezes.

"Do I need to hurt you to make you come?" he asks, pulling out and thrusting in hard. The movement steals my breath away. I cup the back of his head with my hand and twist my fingers into his hair. One corner of his mouth curves up.

"Say it. Tell me."

With his other hand, he bends one leg up. His next thrust is deeper and harder and the next one harder still.

"More," I say, my eyes closing.

"Open. Look at me."

I do. I reach up to kiss him. "Hurt me," I say into his mouth. "I need it."

He takes my arms and spreads them wide. Our fingers are intertwined, and he's fucking me and looking at me and kissing me—and I'm going to come. Just from his eyes alone, the way he looks at me, the way he sees me, I'm going to come, and he knows it. I feel him too; he's moving faster and deeper, and his breath is ragged, as ragged as mine. When I feel him thicken and I watch him as he dips his head down and bites my lip, I squeeze my eyes shut, and I come. I'm gripping his hands, gripping him because I can't let go. I won't know how to be if I let go, not after this. Not anymore after this.

When I open my eyes again, I find him watching me and as the last of my orgasm fades away, all I can think is that he's wrong.

That there is more of me to break.

8

GIOVANNI

We're sitting at the dining-room table where dinner is laid out. According to the cook, Emilia didn't eat today. She's so fucking stubborn. She's on her second plate of curry now. I'm going to guess all that whiskey on an empty stomach is part of the reason for the fucked-up emotions out there. That, and the panic when I threw her into the pool. I have to admit, seeing her like that, beneath the surface, going down, panic in her eyes but not the fight I'd expect, not that instinctual fight to survive—I don't like it.

I know why she didn't put on the dress I sent earlier. She's only wearing it now because she has no choice, since her dress is soaked. It's a pretty, frilly yellow summer dress, and it leaves part of her back exposed. The silvery lines begin crisscrossing at the tops of her shoulder blades, and I know they go all the way to her lower back. Twenty-one lines, some thick, badly healed, others flat to the skin.

When she glances sideways at me, I slide a forkful of chicken into my mouth but don't take my eyes off her.

"Who did it?"

"You know what?" She drops her fork on her plate. "It's none of your business. They're old. They're nothing."

"Your father?"

"No! God, no, he would never! He never raised a hand to me. Not once."

"Your brother?"

She shoves her chair back and stands. "I'm done. I want to go home."

"Sit down." I eat another bite, feeling pretty calm. I know the answer. She's just given it to me. But the who isn't as important as the why.

"Just let me go."

Same request as when she was in the pool. *Let me go.* Thing is, I don't think she wants me to let her go.

And I don't want to let her.

"Why did he do it?"

"You're stubborn," she says, but she sits and picks up her fork to push food around her plate.

"Only as stubborn as you. You don't want to tell me?"

"No."

"You will. In time." I take a sip of my beer. "Had an interesting day today."

"Why would I care?"

"I think you will. Met a man who used to work for your brother."

She glances at me but is quick to look away.

"Well, he worked for your dad first. Liked him better, he said. That was before he was killed, obviously."

"Who?"

"John Diaz."

Her back goes rigid.

"Did you know he's married now? Has a kid." I take the

last bite of my chicken, wipe my mouth, and sit back to enjoy the rest of my beer.

"I don't know him," she says finally.

"No? He knows you. Got a strange look on his face when I mentioned you."

"Why would you mention me?"

"Just making conversation."

"Why?"

"Because you're a mystery to me."

She finishes eating and drinks the rest of her beer. We sit quietly for a few minutes before she finally asks: "Did he tell you where Alessandro is?'"

"No. He didn't know."

I can see the relief on her face.

"Would you like dessert?" I ask.

"No, thanks."

"Want to talk about your freak-out at the pool?"

"Not really. It's not a big deal." She shrugs. "I just never learned how to swim. I know it sounds stupid, but I'm afraid of deep water if I'm being honest. Always have been."

"Not stupid. What else are you afraid of?"

She watches me calmly. She's so good at this, at hiding any emotion. "That's a strange question."

"Your brother?"

She just holds that smile, and I can't figure her out.

"What about you? What are you afraid of? There has to be something even for someone like you," she asks.

I think about this. I don't think I ever actually have. I shrug a shoulder. "Can't think of anything, honestly. When I was little, I was afraid of my father. He wasn't as gentle as yours seems to have been."

"What did he do?"

"He wanted to be sure my brother and I were tough. Wanted to be sure we were prepared for this life."

"Did he hurt you?"

"Nothing as terrible as he probably wanted to do. I won't carry scars for the rest of my life." She lowers her eyes to her lap for a moment.

"Are you and your brother close?"

"We're not close, but we're not enemies. We like each other well enough. I have a sister too. Half-sister, actually, from one of my father's many affairs."

"How old is she?"

"Seventeen."

"Where does she live?"

"At a boarding school in England. It's her last year. She's a handful." I smile, though. I like Alysia. She's a pain in the ass, but tough. I like her.

"You grew up in Italy?"

"We split our time between southern Italy and New York. You spent most of yours in the states."

She nods but is cautious. I wonder if she's surprised I know. "My dad thought it was safer. Ironic as it is."

"He was probably right."

"Didn't work for him though." The assassination took place when he was in the U.S.

"No, I guess it didn't." My phone vibrates with a text message. Her eyes move to it, as do mine, and I pick it up. It's a text from one of my men.

"It's him."

"Secure the property and her apartment as well," I type back.

"What did you mean when you said I look like her?"

I delete both messages before looking up at her, seeing her

in a different light. Feeling even more curious now than before. I'm trying to work out whether or not it was her who did it. How she would have managed it. Because who else would have saved that bastard's life? Who else would keep him in hiding?

"Did you hear me?" she asks when I don't reply.

I hear her loud and clear. I knew that moment would come back to haunt me. But she gets under my skin. Makes me lose control.

"Nothing. Just wanted to fuck with you." I check my watch. "Time for bed, Emilia."

"What?"

I stand. "Time for bed. Go upstairs."

She pushes back, and I think what I see on her face is close to disappointment. "Can I just go home?"

"Not tonight." My men will be working in her apartment tonight. "I'll be up later."

I walk out of the room without waiting for her to reply. I don't feel like a discussion right now. I have some work to do.

IT'S EARLY THE NEXT MORNING. I'M STANDING OVER EMILIA, putting on my cuff links and watching her sleep. She's pretty when she sleeps. Soft, with her dark hair splayed out around her, her face relaxed, her lips slightly parted. I guess I'm surprised she sleeps so easily here, in my bed.

But what I learned last night, it shows me a whole other side of her. I know she's strong. Of that I have no doubt. But what she's managed to do—who she's managed to hide—I have to say I'm impressed. And even more curious about her secrets because she keeps them well.

When I finish with the cuff links, I go to my closet, pick out a tie, then return to the bed.

"Wake up, Sunshine."

She groans and rolls over away from me. I have to smile as I tuck the tie beneath my collar and lean down toward her.

"Rise and shine."

She stiffens. I straighten, watch her blink her eyes open, see her remember where she is. She rolls over onto her back and pulls the sheet higher, as if just remembering she's naked. She looks up at me, looks at what I'm wearing. I'm knotting my tie, watching her.

"What do you want?"

"You're not a morning person, are you? Although you don't seem to be much of a night person either."

"Maybe it's you. Maybe you just bring out the worst in me."

"Maybe." I check my watch. "Get up. We leave for Mass in thirty minutes, so we have time to drop by your apartment for something appropriate for you to wear."

"Mass?" She sits up a little, obviously confused by this.

"That's what I said."

"Why?"

"What does that mean?"

"It means why do *you* go to Mass? Considering...who you are."

I shrug a shoulder. "I was raised Catholic. It was important to my mother, and I guess it stuck. So, let's go. Up."

She holds the blanket up to cover her chest and swings her legs over the bed. "I haven't been to church since I was a kid," she says, climbing out of bed and wrapping the blanket around her. She walks toward the bathroom but stops at the door and turns. "This is weird, you know that, right?"

I shrug a shoulder. "Thirty minutes." I leave her and head downstairs, sit down at the dining-room table, and drink some coffee while checking messages. Twenty minutes later, Emilia appears downstairs, freshly showered and wearing the pretty yellow dress from last night. She looks over the breakfast table.

"Have a seat."

"Aren't you supposed to abstain from food before Communion?" she asks, sitting down.

"I think God would forgive you if you ate breakfast." I pour her a mug of coffee.

She takes it, adds a little sugar and a generous amount of cream. "Thank you," she says, taking a sip.

I reach for the toast and butter a slice. "Are you seriously not going to eat for religious reasons?"

She smiles. "No. I never eat breakfast first thing. Just coffee."

The toast crunches when I bite into it. "Suit yourself." A text comes through. I shift my attention back to my phone but feel her watching me.

"Both properties are secured."

I reply with a thanks, finish my toast, and turn to her. "Ready?"

She takes another sip of coffee, then nods and stands.

Vincent is already waiting with the car. A few minutes later, we're on our way to her apartment.

"Do you really go to mass every Sunday?"

"Yes. Why is that so strange to you?"

"Well, you're...the mafia."

"I thought you'd have had a strong religious upbringing."

She shakes her head. "Nan, the woman who raised us, would take Alessandro and me to church now and again, but my dad never went. Said it was pointless. Said if there was a God, what happened wouldn't have happened."

"What do you think?"

She startles at my question. I guess she's surprised I'm asking it. But when she answers, it's very matter-of-factly. "I think he's right."

I don't really like her answer. No, not so much her answer, but more how she answered. But I drop it when we pull up to her apartment a few minutes later.

"I don't have my keys," she says, as if just remembering we didn't stop to pick up her bag after the incident at the club.

I take out mine. "I have mine."

"Why do you have keys to my apartment?"

"Aren't you glad I do?" I answer and open the front door, gesture for her to enter.

She mutters something under her breath and heads up. I follow her up the six flights of stairs and unlock her door.

"You'll give those back when this is finished?" I know she wants it to sound like a statement of fact, but it comes out more a question.

I give her a smile and reach for my phone. "Hurry up. I don't like being late."

When she emerges fifteen minutes later, she's wearing a pretty pink sleeveless dress and matching pumps. She drops a lipstick into the clutch she's holding, and her hair is in its usual, perfect bun.

"You look good," I say. It's awkward.

"Thanks." She clears her throat.

"Let's go."

The chapel I go to is closer to the Lincoln property, but I make the trip every Sunday. My mom used to bring us here when we were little, and although there are a hundred churches in the city, this is the one I want to be at.

We arrive at the small stone structure forty-five minutes later. It's old and beautiful and the scent of incense already permeates the air as we near the arched wooden door. A nun walks in ahead of us, looking over her shoulder to pass the door to us. She gives a nod of acknowledgement but not quite a smile. I guess she wonders, too, why I bother. I'm hell bound. There is no god willing to forgive the likes of me.

But when we step inside, the familiar notes of the organ soothe me, make me forget the nun. I don't care what she thinks. What anyone thinks. I am who I am, and if they don't like it, they can go fuck themselves. Besides, if it weren't for my generosity, this church wouldn't still be standing.

I dip my fingers in holy water and make the sign of the cross, the music already carrying me back in time. The sensation is almost tangible.

Emilia follows my lead with the holy water, surprising me. Only about half of the pews are occupied. I guide Emilia to one near the back. Father Germain, the ancient priest, is at the pulpit. I remember him from when I was little.

The mass is said in Italian, which I know surprises Emilia, but she is silent. I watch her watching the priest, listening intently. I wonder if she can follow or if this is meaningful for her at all.

It's not until much later, when she walks down the aisle and toward the altar for communion, surprising me again, that the church door opens. It isn't until then that the feeling of well-being dissipates and is replaced by something cold.

I hear Vincent say something, hear a woman reply. Then I hear him.

I turn to the entrance, and I know Emilia is coming back down the aisle without having to see her for myself. I know because my father's eyes are tracking her. They take in every inch of her. They fucking devour her. His lecherous gaze makes my hands fist. I feel how my face hardens, how my jaw sets. Janet's looking at me, her expression one of trepidation, of anxious anticipation. He made her bring him. I know it instantly.

My father smiles when Emilia reaches the pew. She knows something is up, and I think she guesses who he is. I step into the aisle for her to enter, placing one more barrier between him and her.

The organ booms, but I still hear my father order Janet to push his wheelchair toward us. Father Germain gives his final blessing, and the altar boys begin to walk down the aisle to the back of the church. They pass us, followed by Father Germain and more altar boys. The whole while, my father's eyes are locked on Emilia. All I can do is wrap one of my hands around the back of her neck. Pull her closer.

Because my father is just as dangerous for her as I am.

Because this time, the girl is mine.

9

EMILIA

I know the old man in the wheelchair is Giovanni's father.

The church slowly empties. The priest and altar boys leave, and the organ music dies down. The parishioners begin to speak in hushed tones as they make their way out of the church. A baby cries. The mother walks quickly by, the child in her arms. The father and another, older child, follow them out. I do notice the glances we get by most, if not all.

Giovanni's hand tightens possessively around the back of my neck as he steps out of the aisle, moving me with him. Vincent approaches but remains standing behind the old man and the woman I assume is his nurse. She looks anxious. More than anxious. But the man is grinning from ear to ear and tells the woman to push him forward. She's reluctant, but a moment later, we meet in the aisle.

"What the hell are you doing here?" Giovanni asks, his tone curt.

The man in the chair looks up at Giovanni, his expression shifting, the smile fading into surprise. But I can see it's an act.

"Watch your language. We're in a holy place."

"Since when have you cared about that? Since when do you come to Mass?"

The old man turns to me, a smile back on his face. I can see a slight resemblance, but not so much that I'd pick them out to be related if I didn't already know.

"I came to meet Emilia."

My name on his tongue sends a shiver down my spine. How does he know about me? "What?"

"I knew he'd never bring you to the house, so I thought I'd better pop in here. My son is quite predictable. He never misses Mass. But between you and me, if it's redemption he seeks, I think he'll be disappointed." The old man extends his hand to me. "My dear, I'm Antonio Santa Maria, Giovanni's father."

I feel Giovanni fuming beside me. I'm not sure what to do. I extend my hand, but before it reaches the old man's, Giovanni captures my wrist, stopping me. Without taking his eyes from the old man, he steps between us, keeping hold of my wrist, almost using his body as a barrier between me and his father.

"If you touch her, I will cut off your hand."

The words make me gasp, but the old man doesn't seem to be at all impacted. In fact, his grin widens. I see the hate between them. Father and son.

It makes me think of my father and brother. Life is so strange. It's like things keep appearing, keep repeating. Like there's one theme, and life keeps shoving it in your face.

Mr. Santa Maria puts his hand back on his lap. "Sadly, I believe you would."

"Giovanni," I start.

"Vincent," he calls, cutting me off. Vincent arrives, and he hands me off to him. "Take her to the car. I'll be out in a minute."

I go, only because I don't know what else to do. But the old man meets my eyes as I go and gives me a smile, an almost apologetic one. The door to the church closes but just before it does, I hear Giovanni's voice. The threat in it makes me shudder.

A few minutes later, Giovanni appears. His face is unreadable as he walks toward the car. Vincent meets him a few steps away, says something and I see Giovanni's gaze shift to another vehicle parked a little farther away in the lot. He changes direction. I watch as he stalks toward it, toward the man who steps out of the driver's seat. He's big, this guy. Almost as big as Giovanni. He closes the door and squares his shoulders, the look in his eyes hard as stone.

I open my door, but Vincent tells me to stay inside and closes it. He resumes watching the interaction between the men.

Giovanni goes right up to the man, there's not a second of hesitation. The man says something and stands immobile beside the sedan with its dark-tinted windows. I wish I could hear what was being said. When I see Giovanni poke a finger in the guy's chest and lean in close, I know he's issuing a threat. My mind can't help but wander to what he said to his father.

"If you touch her, I will cut off your hand."

If he touches me, Giovanni will cut off his hand. Is this because of what happened with his tutor? Because his father slept with her?

A few minutes later, he's back and in the car. I feel the rage coming off him. I remain silent, watching him. His face is set, eyes straight ahead. He's fuming.

"Take her home," he says, giving the instruction to Vincent.

"Home?" I guess I don't expect him to let me walk away like that.

I don't want to say I'm let down. I'm not. It's not disappointment at all. Just surprise.

But maybe he's already tired of me. I should be glad. It's what I want.

He glances at me. "Don't tell me you don't want to go home."

"Yes, but... What happened in there?"

"Nothing that concerns you."

"You threatened to cut off your father's hand if he touched me."

He just watches me.

"Why would you do that?"

"You don't know our history, Emilia. What you think you know—that's not it."

"Then explain it to me."

He takes a long time before he answers. "Trust me, this is in your best interest."

"I don't understand—"

"It's not for you to understand." We don't speak again until we're parked outside my building. "Pack a bag. I'll send someone for you in a few hours. In the meantime, you're not to leave your apartment."

"What? Why not? You can't just bring my world to a standstill."

"Believe it or not, Emilia, it's to keep you safe."

"What, this is in my best interest too?"

He reads a text message on his phone, ignoring me.

"I need to work," I say.

"Pack your work things, then." Vincent opens the door.

Giovanni is busy with whatever new message he's reading. "Vincent will walk you up."

"That's it? You're not going to tell me anything else?"

He stops reading, looks at me, and cocks his head to the side. "Do you tell me anything, Emilia?" I don't reply. "Exactly. Don't leave the apartment, understand?"

I just snort and step out of the car.

Vincent walks me up to my apartment and even sweeps it before leaving. I'm surprised he's allowing me to stay here alone because part of me knows I'm safest at Giovanni's house. But then again, he probably has a man stationed outside.

Once I'm alone, the first thing I do is search through my kitchen drawers to find the old phone I keep as a backup. I've never had to use it before, but since I don't have my purse, I'm glad I always kept this one. But it's a couple of years old, and it needs to be charged before I can even turn it on. I plug it into the wall and locate my spare keys. I make some food while I wait, wishing it were later in the day, wanting the cover of darkness.

I do as Giovanni said and pack some things, then change into running clothes and put on a baseball cap, pulling my hair through it. I tuck some cash into my armband. Once the phone is charged, I stick the headphones onto my ears, but nothing is playing. I just want the man Giovanni has following me to believe I'm going out for a jog. It was easy enough to lose him last time. I doubt I'll have an issue now, even though it's daytime.

I walk out the door and tuck the key into the pocket in my shorts. I look up and down the street when I get outside, pretending to stretch as I scan for the soldier. He's in his car a little ways down the street.

A few minutes later, I hop down the stairs and move into

a steady jog, warming up my muscles gently as I navigate the pedestrian-filled streets. I know the man in the car is following me, but I'll lose him at the next street.

When that light turns green, I drop down, pretending to tie my laces. I take my time as cars honk their horns, forcing the driver through the intersection. He'll wait at the next block, I'm sure, but when the light turns red, I pop into the coffee shop on the corner and exit through the side door, where I hurry through the narrow alley and come out on another busy street. From there, I cross two more city blocks before hailing a taxi and giving him the address. I'm out of breath when I glance behind me, but I'm pretty sure I've lost him. And if I haven't already, I will in the sea of yellow taxis. I take out my phone and dial Nan. I never make this call from home. It's a rule for myself. Even if Alessandro found me, I won't take the chance he'll find what I'm hiding.

Nan answers on the second ring.

"Emilia, honey? Is that you?"

"Hi, Nan. How are you?"

"Oh, honey, I'm so glad you called. I've been so worried all day." She's alarmed, which immediately makes me nervous

"What is it? Is everything okay?"

"I don't know, baby. There were some men here today."

"Who? Is dad—"

"He's fine," she stops, corrects herself. "Same." Because he's not fine. "I tried to call you."

"I didn't have my phone. I'm sorry. Was it Alessandro?" To say his name makes me shudder. To think of him finding our father in the state he's in terrifies me. It terrifies me more than him coming for me does.

"No. I don't know who they were, but they're gone now."

"Did they hurt him?"

"No. He's the same, honey. They didn't touch him. But they know it's him. I'm sure."

"Okay. I'm heading out there right now. Sit tight."

"No, baby girl. Don't come here. If it's your brother—"

"I'm not leaving you alone there. If it is Alessandro's men, then he's on his way too. I'm not leaving you unprotected."

"Who will protect you?" Her tone is sharp.

"I'll see you soon."

The taxi pulls up a few blocks away from the old house, and I pay the driver. This is a quiet part of town on the outskirts of the city. Not much foot traffic here and fewer yellow cabs. I look around cautiously as I exit and go around the block, breaking into a jog and having to work hard not to sprint. I don't want to attract attention to myself, although I know my secret is no longer safe. Someone's found me out. I just have to hope it's not Alessandro.

Who else would it be though?

Nan is waiting for me at the door. The lights downstairs are out except for the kitchen, which is around back. We go directly there. I take off my cap and the armband that holds my phone and set them both on the table.

"I made us some tea."

"Thank you. I'll be right there." I take a look around the house, although I'm not sure what I'm expecting to find. It doesn't look like anyone turned the place upside down, but there's no reason to be here but to find him. And he can't hide. He can barely move on his own.

The door to my father's room is open a crack. The window shades are drawn and the lights from the machines cast a dim, unnatural glow over him. I push the door open, listen to the familiar squeak of the hinges, the low hum of the machines. I step inside, smile a bittersweet smile when I look at him, even though he can't see me. He's sound asleep. He's always sound asleep. I tuck the blanket up a little closer, ignoring the tubes, pretending they're not there at all, and lean down to kiss his forehead, then brush a few wisps of white hair back from his face. He looks so much older than he is. We just celebrated his fifty-sixth birthday. But for anyone who doesn't know him, to look at him now you'd think a man of eighty lay in the bed.

I feel Nan enter behind me. She rubs my back and gestures for me to go with her. I do, and she closes the door behind us.

"He's okay. I don't think they even touched him," she says. We speak in English, we always have, the breaks in her words are familiar and comforting. Nan has been in my life for as long as I can remember. She was our surrogate mother. She raised Alessandro and I, traveling with us between Mexico and the states. Nan only left when we were in our late teens and didn't need watching. By then her daughter had had her own baby, and she'd come to New York City to help her. I don't think she ever expected things to end up like this. My father helpless and in her care. My brother the one responsible.

The night of the shooting, I'd been home. I wasn't supposed to be, and I am sure that's what saved us both. Masked men broke into our house, killing most of the staff before going after my father. I'd been in the attic, looking for old birthday decorations to surprise him the following morning. I wasn't expected until two days later, but I'd finished my work early. I'd decided to surprise my dad.

I remember the sound of gunfire, automatic weapons mowing down every man, woman, and child in the house, on the property. They even killed the unarmed women and the smallest children. No one thought to check the attic where I hid. Where, I'm ashamed to say, I cowered. But I had no weapon, and I too would have been killed if I'd come out of hiding.

I still don't know if it was Alessandro himself who shot my father. I don't know if it was him or his men. And although I had no doubt that Alessandro was behind the assassination, him telling me what he did, admitting that it was him before he did what he did to me, it made me hate him. I don't think I did hate him until then.

By then he'd been gone for three years. I knew of the bad blood between him and my father but never suspected it had gone so far. Never realized it was different than when we were kids. That the damage Alessandro could do was much more deadly now.

But when they set the house on fire, the house where we grew up, that's when I came out of the attic. My father, miraculously, wasn't dead yet. I found him on the floor behind his desk in his study, gunned down but breathing, and somehow, I got us both out of the house, glad the assassins had run off to celebrate. They hadn't waited to watch the house burn, watch all those memories turn to ash. That was a godsend. I managed to get us to safety, to a doctor who my father trusted. He kept him hidden and tended to his wounds. We knew right away there was no hope for him. He would live, but the bullet to the head, it had taken away the essence of the man I knew as my father. Still, I couldn't abandon him.

Nan and I sit down at the kitchen table, and she pours us both a cup of tea. The smell of it takes me back. Back to a happy time. But a look at her face tells me she's afraid.

"Tell me everything."

"They came in the morning. Three men. Americans, or

at least they spoke English like Americans. Dark hair and olive skin, but not Mexican."

"You're sure?"

She nods.

"Then not Alessandro's men?"

"I don't know. Italian maybe?"

"Italian?"

"Maybe. They rang the doorbell, and when I opened the door, one man smiled at me, said his name but too quickly and they all move inside, the man smiling taking my hands and holding them but making sure I know I should do as he says." She stops to sip her tea, and I see how she's aged today. How the lines on her face are a little deeper. I can't do this to her. I can't expect her to put herself in danger to take care of my comatose father.

"I'm sorry, Nan. I shouldn't have left you here on your own unprotected. I'm so sorry."

"No, child. I love that man like my own family." She cups my head, strokes my hair. "You are like my own daughter."

"Go on with your story, Nan."

She nods, takes another sip of tea before continuing. "The men, they looked around the house. They all wore dark suits, and I knew they had guns because I saw one under the jacket of the man who was sitting with me, talking about something but I don't know what. He was trying to keep me calm, I think. They don't want a hysterical old woman shrieking, I suppose."

"I suppose."

"When they found your father, I started to tell them he was my brother. Asked them what they wanted with him. But they ignored me and take a few photographs and the whole time, your father just lay there like he does. God bless him. I thought they would hurt him, but they left. They simply said good-bye and told me to lock my doors tight and left."

I rub my shoulder, the back of my neck. I'm tense, everything feels stiff. "They never said who they were? Didn't leave anything?"

She shakes her head.

"I think if it was Alessandro's men, they would have hurt him."

"But who else? We have to get him out of here. I'll make arrangements as soon as possible. I'll stay here with you tonight. Do you still have the gun I gave you?"

She points to the kitchen drawer and nods. "I won't use that. And you shouldn't either."

I get up, open the drawer, take it out, and check that it's loaded. "I will if I have to. I'm not going to let anyone hurt us."

I spend the day thinking about all my options, weighing everything, knowing I have exactly one. By the time I decide to do it, we've already had dinner and it's late. "Why don't you go up to bed. I just need to make a few calls."

I have to think about this as an acceleration of my own plans. I meant to come here today to tell my father and Nan that I'd be leaving. That I'd be having my father moved as soon as I settled somewhere. But now, I have to do things differently. I have to get him to safety first. Get Nan to her own family. And maybe I can't leave. Maybe I have to pay the devil. Maybe I have to accept Giovanni's help. His protection. But will he help me when he sees what I'm hiding? Who I'm hiding? Even if my father is no longer the head of the Estrella cartel, they are far from friends.

But I have no choice.

I get up, say a silent prayer in the hopes that I'm doing the right thing, and pick up the house phone to dial Giovanni's phone number. He answers on the second ring, and I'm surprised when he knows it's me.

"Good run?" he asks. He knows that too.

But it doesn't matter anymore.

"I need your help."

10

GIOVANNI

I'm standing outside the house at the address I found in John Diaz's pocket. It's where Emilia has been keeping her father hidden for the last four years. I wonder how she's done it. How she's kept her secret. Saved his life. What's left of it.

The door opens, and Emilia stands there looking reluctantly up at me.

I smile down at her. I like her like this. In my debt. Needing me. Needing my help. My protection.

She steps aside, and I enter along with several of my men, who split up throughout the house. She closes the door, and I glance around the large, old space, then back to her. I cock my head to the side.

"Don't gloat," she says.

"That's not a very nice welcome, considering I've just driven across town at your request."

"We need to talk terms before I accept any offer."

I chuckle. "I make the terms, Sunshine, and you already made the offer. Now first, thank me for coming out of my way especially when I clearly told you to stay put."

It takes her a long minute, but finally, she drops her gaze and says it. "Thank you."

"You're welcome. Just know there will be payment later. Where is he?" I move around her, but she catches my arm. He eyes betray her alarm.

"You're not going to hurt him, right? I mean, he's harmless. He's not the head of the cartel anymore, Giovanni."

I look down at where she's gripping my forearm. "Where is he?"

When she turns, I notice something bulgy in her tight running clothes and halt her by grabbing her arm.

"You can't think I'm this stupid," I say, tugging her shirt up and taking the pistol.

"I didn't put it there for you. I wasn't sure who'd been here this afternoon. If it was Alessandro."

"Still, I'll hold on to this. You don't have a good track record. Do I need to strip search you? Are you hiding anything else?"

She looks down at herself and gives me an incredulous look. "Where do you think I'd manage to hide something?"

I give her a one-sided grin. "I don't know. You're a tricky one."

"I'm not hiding any more weapons. I promise."

"Take me to your father."

I follow her to a room at the back of the house, making a mental map of the property as I pass through. Once we get to the door, she stops, turns to me, and looks like she's going to say something. Instead she changes her mind and pushes the door open.

The room is simple with not a single picture or poster on the walls. The curtain is drawn over the one small window, and a large hospital bed sits in the center with an old man sleeping on it, hooked up to several machines. He doesn't stir when Emilia enters. She goes to him and takes his hand.

I follow her in. Earlier today, I'd seen the photos my men sent. It had taken us some time to confirm it was him. He's a shadow of the man he'd been. Emil Estrella was a force to be reckoned with. This sleeping man is simply an old man. Not a threat. Not even close.

When I look at her, she's watching me.

Just then, there's a commotion in the hallway. Instinctively, I draw my weapon and push Emilia behind me as she tries to slip past me and into the hall. An old woman is standing half-way down the stairs. Emilia exhales and closes the door as quietly as she can before going to her.

"It's okay, Nan. I called these men. They're going to help us."

I look at Nan as she looks at each of the men. A moment later, she whispers something to Emilia. When Emilia turns to me, it's with fisted hands and rage in her eyes.

"It was you?"

"What?" I play dumb.

"The men who were here earlier, it was your men?"

I give her a wide grin, take my eyes off her for a second to holster my weapon and next thing I know, she's coming at me, arm raised. I'm ready when the flat of her hand collides with my face.

There's a gasp from behind her. It's the old woman.

The sting of the slap is nothing like the heat of rage that burns through me.

I narrow my eyes, and Emilia steps back. I see her throat work as she swallows. She hesitated at the last moment, so it wasn't a hard slap, but it was still a slap and she'll need to be dealt with. I take the wrist of the offending arm and twist it. "You'll pay for that later."

There's a flicker of apprehension in her eyes, but she doesn't retort. That's good. Best to handle this in private.

"I called you to help me, and you knew all along?"

"I tried to tell you. Remember my mention of your friend, Diaz, at dinner?"

"He's not my friend."

"You weren't interested in hearing."

"Wait, he told you about my father? He knew?" Her face goes white. She's just understood what this means.

I shift my grip so I have both of her wrists in one hand and turn to one of my men. "I had a message that the house was secured earlier. How many are staying the night?"

"Yes, sir," the man says. "House is secure, has been all day, and we have four men on property."

"Good. Let's get the old man moved tomorrow. I'll make arrangements and send the location in the morning."

"What?" Emilia is asking.

I turn to her. "Nan, is it?" I ask, gesturing to the old woman. "Nan, I'm Giovanni Santa Maria. My men will be on site tonight. I don't expect trouble, but if there is, they'll keep you and Mr. Estrella safe. I'm taking Emilia with me."

"Wait, no. I'm not going anywhere."

"If you need to contact her, ask one of my men," I say, ignoring Emilia's tugging.

The old woman looks at Emilia then at me and says something in Spanish.

Before Emilia can answer, I do, in Spanish. The language is close to Italian and one I studied growing up. I tell her to do as she's told and that everything and everyone will be fine if she does. I also add in that I'm not going to let anything happen to Emilia. At this, she gives me a nod, comes down the stairs toward Emilia, wraps her arms around her, and whispers for her not to fight me. She then turns and goes back up the stairs.

"What are you doing?" Emilia asks.

"I'm helping you like you asked me to." I begin to walk us toward the door, but she's resisting.

"But this isn't what I asked for."

"The moment you asked for my help, you gave up control of the situation to me. I make the terms, you simply accept them. That's how it works."

"No, that's not—"

"Let's go."

"Where are we going?"

"To bed. I'm tired."

"I don't want to leave them."

I turn to her, take her by the shoulders. "They're safe, Emilia. I promise to keep them safe."

"Wait, what did you mean about Diaz? What did he know about my father?"

"He was one of the men hired to assassinate him originally. I guess your brother figured out your father was still alive and considered the job not yet done, so Diaz was coming after him. He had the address in his pocket. That's how I found the house. I've had it under surveillance all day, expecting Alessandro. Hoping he'd turn up. Imagine my surprise when I got you instead."

"My brother."

I lean down close to her. "You do as you're told, and I promise I will not let him hurt you or them, understand?"

"But what about you? You hate my father. You hate the cartel."

"I guess you're going to have to trust me. Now let's go. We've still got some matters to resolve between us."

Her eyes search mine. She knows I'm talking about that

slap. She doesn't fight me when I take her out to the car. She's lost in her thoughts, and I'm busy confirming arrangements, so we don't talk on the drive home. We get to the house and enter through the kitchen. I put my phone away.

"Go upstairs to my room and wait for me there. You remember which one it is?"

"Can we just get this over with?"

"Get what over with?"

"You know what."

I raise my eyebrows. Her back is to the counter.

"Do you want to slap me back or something?"

I take a step to her, and she scoots around me. I smile, stalk toward her.

"Don't test me. Do as you're told."

She stands defiant. "Just do it. If that's what you're going to do."

I study her. She's got her arms folded across her chest, and her head is tilted to the side. Her chin is set in a stubborn and, quite frankly, stupid, challenge.

Whatever she sees in my eyes, though, makes her falter. When I take one more step, she takes another one back.

"I don't slap women, Emilia, but I do have a special punishment in mind for you. Now go upstairs, and wait for me there. Make sure you're naked. It'll save us time."

She swallows, and I see her cheeks flush, but I also see her need to stand her ground.

To defy me.

"No."

"Emilia." I take one final step and when she matches it, her back hits the wall so she has to crane her neck to look up at me. Her face is flushed, and the rapid rise and fall of her chest belies her anxiety. I reach out, push a stray hair back from her face, and touch her cheek with the back of my hand. I'm gentle, and she's soft. So fucking soft. My gaze holds hers as I run my hand down over her jaw, her delicate, vulnerable throat, lightly touching her collarbone before sliding it to the back of her neck, cupping the back of her head.

Her pupils are dilating, her eyes darker but for the thin ring of green. She licks her lips. Although I'm sure it's involuntary, sure she's not aware how she looks. How she's looking at me. I wonder if she has any idea how much her body is giving away.

"You don't listen very well," I whisper, leaning in closer so I can smell her, feel the warmth of her skin on mine. Feel that charge, that almost electrical spark when we touch. "But I like bad girls." I grip her tight ponytail, see her wince as I tug her head backward. I hold her like that, watching her face, watching the tear at the corner of one eye. Waiting for it to fall. Squeezing harder until it does. Until I'm satisfied.

I open my mouth and lick that tear. Taste the salty droplet as she gasps in surprise, and my dick's hard.

I bring my mouth to hers, touch my lips to hers, inhale before kissing her. She makes a sound—a surprised gasp—and I deepen the kiss, let my tongue slide between her full lips to lick hers, to taste her. Her eyes close but I'm still watching her. I tug on her hair and tilt her head farther and kiss her deeper and fuck, I want her. I want to fuck her right here.

But she needs to be punished first.

A low growl leaves my chest, and I break the kiss. Her eyes flutter open, pupils fully dilated so they look almost black. I grin, rub the scruff of my jaw against her arrogant cheekbone, inhale close to her ear so she hears me.

"You're turned on."

She opens her mouth to deny it, but I continue. She's perfectly still. I'm sure she's holding her breath.

I like it. Like her like this. Like being this close to her. Fuck, I like her scared and defiant and at my mercy. It makes me fucking hard.

It's sick, I know, but as much as pain gets her off, this is what gets me off.

"I see it. And I smell it."

"You're wrong," she says, but her voice is a whisper. "Let me go."

"You don't want me to let you go."

"I do."

"You like the idea of me punishing you?"

"Let me go," she repeats, her voice wavering. I feel her small hands on my chest, trying, but failing, to put space between us.

"You like it? Your dirty mind imagining what I'll do?" I squeeze my fist tighter, tugging on her hair until she lets out a small cry. "If I'll fuck your ass again. Hurt you but make you come so hard you pass out?"

"Stop it."

"I'll tell you a secret," I say, taking my time, breathing in her fear, her arousal. "We're two peas in a pod, you and me." She makes a sound, and I press against her. "See, hurting you gets me off."

Her hands are on my chest, and she shoves against me. "You're sick."

"If I'm sick, what are you?" I ask, looking down at her.

"Stop it."

"No need to hide it. No need to be ashamed of it, not with me," I say, pressing my erection against her belly. She whines, but when I slide one hand between her legs and rub her sex, that whine turns into a low moan of desire.

I realize I've still got a fistful of her hair when more tears fall from her eyes. I feel them on my cheek and pull back, look down at her. She can't hold my gaze.

"Am I right? Are you turned on thinking about what I'm going to do to you?"

"Stop."

"I'll tell you what. I won't keep you in suspense any longer," I say, using her hair to turn her around so her back is to me and the side of her cheek is to the wall. Keeping her like that, I slap her ass, making her jump, then dig my fingers into the fleshy mound.

"I'm going to spank that sweet ass of yours, but it won't be the erotic kind."

I let go of her ponytail and step back. The instant I do, she does exactly what I know she will. She runs. And I smile. Because the chase is on. And I do love the chase.

"Come back here and take your punishment, Emilia," I say, stalking after her.

"Stay away from me!" She's in the living room, standing on the opposite end of the sofa.

"Here," I say, pointing to the arm of the couch. "Now."

Her eyes slide to where I'm pointing. She shakes her head.

"Come over here. Come take your punishment."

"No. You're a freak!"

"You like it, admit it. Besides, you earned this one, and I'm losing my patience. I won't ask again. If I have to make you take it, I may not let you come afterwards."

"I only hit you because you lied."

"I didn't lie. I tried to tell you, in fact. You're just too stubborn to listen."

"That's not true."

I point to the couch again, and she shakes her head.

"Please don't. I'll go upstairs, like you said."

"Too late for that, Sunshine." And while she stands there hesitating, I close the distance between us and take hold of her before she can run. She lets out a scream as I push her over the arm of the sofa so her face is in the cushions and her ass is high. I draw her running shorts and panties down to expose that perfect little ass.

"Ready?"

"No!"

But I start anyway, spanking her ass with my bare hand, watching her pretty, unmarked flesh turn pink, then red. I spank her hard. I concentrate on one spot until she's wriggling before moving to another spot. It's a hand spanking, but it's still painful. I could do worse, but I won't use my belt on her. Not after I've seen her back.

She meets each spank with a cry. After this, she'll know not to raise a hand to me again.

"Please stop! It's enough."

"Is it?" I ask, smacking the crease between ass and thigh.

She nods. "I'm sorry. Please stop. Please. I really am sorry."

I pause. Wait.

"I'm sorry I hit you." I look down at her. Her cheek is resting on the cushion. Her eyes are open, but she's looking straight ahead, not at me. She's out of breath, and sweat covers her forehead. "I didn't want to hit you."

"Why did you?"

She shakes her head, closes her eyes. "I don't know. You just...you make me feel so out of control."

"Maybe you need to learn to let it go. Give it up to me."

I cup her ass. She sucks in a breath, but I knead it. Her skin is hot, and my dick is so fucking hard, I'm going to blow. When I draw her apart, I see how slick she is and grin.

She doesn't know yet that her punishment has only just begun.

I help her stand, and she gasps when I toss her over my shoulder and carry her upstairs to my bedroom, where I drop her on my bed and climb on top of her as I pull first her sport top off, then my own shirt, popping buttons in my haste, sending them flying across the room.

Her hands are around my neck. I kiss her and cup her ass, swallowing that hiss of pain when I do. I pull her to the edge of the bed, slide to my knees between her legs, and wrap my arms around the backs of her knees, drawing her to me, drawing her pussy to my mouth because I need to taste her. To eat her up. Devour her whole.

She's writhing and moaning as I suck her clit and finger her pussy, her ass, but I'm not ready to let her come yet. She didn't do as she was told, and she won't be coming tonight at all, in fact.

I pull back, wipe the back of my arm over my mouth as I stand, undo my jeans, and push them off. She's up on her elbows watching me, her legs spread wide, her hungry cunt glistening, waiting impatiently to be fucked.

I reach for her hair, which has come out of its ponytail, so I can grip a handful of that thick mass. I drag her to her knees and bring her mouth to my cock. She opens because she's fucking greedy, and I decide to fuck her face, her pretty face, make her choke on my cock because her tears, they only make me harder.

She's got her arms wrapped around my thighs and is gasping for breath, but I don't let up.

"Look up. At me. I want to watch you swallow my cum."

She does. She turns those serpentine eyes up to mine and fuck she's beautiful even with tears streaming down her face, her mouth full of my cock, her tongue wet and hot, her fingernails digging into me when I push too deep, cut off her windpipe. A moment later, I'm all the way in and I throb and I come hard. I fill her up, and she's swallowing what I'm giving her. I feel her throat working and fuck, I like fucking her face.

When I pull her off, she gasps for breath as I draw her to stand by her hair and kiss her dirty little mouth, swallow the cum she couldn't, one hand cupping her sweet, punished ass, fingers digging into it as she moans into my mouth, trying to wrap her leg around me like her arms are around my shoulders. Wanting to come.

I draw back, give her a wicked grin.

"Punishment isn't over, Sunshine." I push her onto the bed. She bounces once before I catch her wrists and, taking a pair of restraints from the nightstand drawer, I lay her back and bind them together over her head.

"What are you doing?"

I take two more cuffs and walk to the foot of the bed to grab one of her ankles. I bind it to one corner then move to the other side and pull her legs wide before binding her other ankle to the other side.

"Making sure you don't get yourself off while I have a shower."

11

EMILIA

He takes his time in the shower. He's humming some tune in there. I hear that too. Happy as can be. Not a fucking care in the world while I lie here, arms bound over my head, legs spread wide, my ass throbbing from that spanking and the need to come overwhelming.

"I hate you," I call out just as the water switches off.

He appears a moment later, a towel wrapped low around his hips, another in his hand as he rubs his hair dry. My eyes wander over those perfectly cut abs to the trail of hair that disappears beneath the towel. I want him and hate myself for the groan that escapes when I can't close my legs, can't rub them together.

"What's that?" he asks with that smirk I hate so much.

"I said I hate you."

He drops the towel he was drying his hair with so his hair is standing up all around his head. He still looks so fucking perfect, it's killing me. He walks over to me, eyes roaming from my face to my sex and back.

"I don't think your pussy hates me," he says, sitting on the edge of the bed and leaning down to lick my clit.

I whimper and arch my back for more.

But he draws back, puts his fingers into my folds, and smears them over my thigh, leaving a wet trail of hungry, unfulfilled arousal.

"Next time I tell you to bend over and take your punishment, maybe you'll do as you're told."

I tug at my bonds as he stands, drops his towel, and climbs on the bed so his knees are in between my legs. He lays himself on top of me, taking care that some of his weight is on his elbows. He's hard again. I feel him at my belly.

He's grinning and watching me, and I hate that he sees how much I want this. How much I want him. How much I want to come.

"I like fucking your face." He licks my lips as he situates himself. Slowly, he slides into me, my opening slick, gaping for him.

I let out a long moan as he stretches me. He kisses the side of my face, my temple.

"I like fucking your pussy too." He's moving slowly, savoring my humiliation, savoring his pleasure. "And your ass. Fuck, Emilia, your ass is so tight, and you come so fucking hard when I fuck it."

"I hate you."

"Nah, you don't hate me. You want me."

I snap my teeth at him, trying to bite him, but he draws back just far enough to be out of reach.

"I'd have put you on your belly to have access to both holes, but I couldn't trust you not to rub yourself to orgasm on my sheets."

"You already punished me. Why are you doing this?"

I feel him thickening inside me. He's going to come again, and he's going to leave me wanting. Again.

"I already told you. You need to learn to take your punishment. This is me teaching you."

I arch my back, determined to take my pleasure from him, but he draws away. Sitting up on his knees, he draws my hips onto his lap, the bonds just allowing for that, and he fucks me, thrusting deep but slow, moaning with each thrust as he leaves me with nothing but want. Not a moment of relief, not a single instant before he comes again, filling me up, emptying inside me again. And when he pulls out and lays me back on the bed, I feel his cum rush out of me. He watches it. And, like last time, after cleaning himself he returns with a warm washcloth and cleans me. Each stroke is a slow, drawn-out torment.

When he's done, he walks around to his side of the bed and sits down, punches something into his phone before lying down beside me, and turns off the light.

"I can't sleep like this."

"Maybe you'll learn your lesson, then. Good night, Emilia."

With that, he rolls onto his side, splays his arm possessively over me, and within a few minutes, I hear his breath level out and he sleeps, content. Satisfied in every way. Leaving me hungry in every way.

MY SHOULDERS ACHE WHEN I WAKE THE NEXT MORNING, BUT there's another sensation that's drawing me out of sleep.

I hear myself moan and feel something warm and wet on me. A moment later my eyes snap open because he's between my legs, holding my knees wide apart as he sucks my clit. I try to tug at my arms bur remember I'm bound. Although he must have uncuffed my legs while I slept because they're bent around his head.

"Fuck." I suck in a breath and look at his dark head as he moves, licking the length of me.

He straightens then, stopping before I come, and I look up at him. He's standing beside the bed fully dressed in a dark button-down shirt and slacks. My gaze pauses on his hands, and I remember my punishment. Why does that turn me on?

"Good morning, Sunshine." Coffee steams on the nightstand, but that's not what I want right now. "I can't tell you the last time I slept that well."

I groan, and he sets one knee on the bed, slaps my hip.

"Don't be like that." He flips me over onto my belly and draws me up so I'm on my knees, my ass to him.

I'm still because the need from last night, he just brought it raging back.

"I hope you'll remember last night's spanking next time you want to misbehave."

His fingers touch a tender spot on my ass. I go to move, but he stops me. I hear the buckle of his belt, and for a moment, I think he's going to use it. I think he's going to use it on me.

"No!"

He grabs my hip before I can scoot away.

"Shh." He unzips his pants, pushes them down a little to release his ready, thick cock, takes it into his hand. "Punishment is over, Sunshine."

He sets one knee on the bed between mine and pushes my head down as he slides into me, and I arch my back against him. He squeezes my ass in his hands. It hurts, it's sore from last night, but then he starts to move. He slips one hand beneath me and takes my clit between two fingers, and I'm lost. I'm a mess. I don't know how many times I come as he fucks me like that, fucks me so deep I'm dripping down my thighs.

I feel his hand in my hair then, his fist gripping it, forcing me to crane my neck. Giovanni's eyes are locked on mine, and he's fucking me harder and his face is fierce, and I know the moment he's going to come. I feel him thicken, I see that glow he gets in his eyes. When he shifts his gaze to watch himself fucking me, watches his cock as it's being swallowed up by my pussy, and he presses his finger into my ass, I explode again as he thrusts to my very core and throbs inside me. When he pulls out, I fall onto the bed limp and empty, my breathing ragged, sweat covering me.

I turn my head to look at him. He stands, wipes his dick off on the towel he'd discarded last night, and tucks himself back into his pants like it was nothing. Like we didn't just fuck like animals. He watches me, sits down on the edge of the bed, and reaches for the key on the nightstand to undo the cuffs on my wrists before he stands again and takes one of the cups of coffee.

"You okay?"

I think he's asking about last night. About the punishment. The fucking. The torment. I don't know exactly, but I nod. I am okay.

He nods too and checks his watch. "Go have a shower. One of my men brought some clothes from your apartment. They're in that bag. Get dressed. Your breakfast is ready in the dining room. Once you've eaten, come into my study. It's time to get some questions answered." He turns and walks to the door.

"Giovanni?"

"Yes?" he asks, turning back to me.

"My father?"

"He's already been moved to a safe location. Nan too."

I exhale. "Thank you."

He just nods like he wasn't expecting that and walks out the door.

12

GIOVANNI

Thirty minutes later, Emilia is sitting in a chair across from my desk. I watch her as she looks around, taking in the large space, the imposing wooden bookcases, the dark walls, heavy curtains. The desk itself is massive, and I know sitting across from it is intimidating. But that's the point.

I get up and walk around the desk. Leaning against it, I fold my arms across my chest.

"Did you eat?"

"Yes. Where are Nan and my father?"

"Safe."

"Where?"

"I'm the one who asks the questions now."

"How can I be sure you won't hurt him?"

"Like I said last night, you'll have to trust me. I'm not sure you have many other options. And I think you already know that, or you wouldn't have asked me for help."

"How long have you known?"

"Only since yesterday."

"Does my brother know yet that Diaz failed again?"

There's a curling to her lip, like there's something distasteful in her mouth.

"I would guess so."

"Are your men at the house? In case they can pick him up there?"

"Yes, but he hasn't been to the house. Not yet. I don't know if he will come. I've also secured your apartment."

The way she looks at me, I know that's where she's expecting him to turn up.

"Is he the one who put those marks on your back?"

She watches me cautiously. I already know the answer, but I want her to confirm it. I want her to know I know.

She nods.

"When?"

"After the attack on my father."

"When he thought he'd killed Emil?"

She nods again. "I was lucky they didn't find my father when they found me a month later. They just assumed he was dead."

I hear her mistake. They. Not he. "Why did they do it?" I ask, curious if she'll pick it up.

She pauses, but I can't read her expression. She doesn't mention the plural. "To punish me."

"Why?"

She looks off, just beyond my shoulder, and it's like she's going back to that time. Her expression is fixed, but I see the emotions flickering through her eyes. The battle she's waging against them on the inside. It takes her a long time to return her gaze to mine.

"Do we really have to do this?"

I nod.

"It's a long, boring story."

"I doubt it's boring."

"Alessandro and I, we aren't twins. We were triplets. Did you know that?"

"No, I didn't." But I do catch her use of the past tense there.

"No one does, I guess. My brother, Stefano, died while we were still inside my mother's belly. We weren't to term yet, but the doctors knew my mother wouldn't be able to carry us that long. But this was still...a surprise.

"When Stefano died, my mom went into premature labor. I was the first one delivered. The only one who came naturally. After me, there were complications, and they had to open her up to get Alessandro and Stefano out. When they did, when they were taking them out, that was when she died. My father lost my mother the instant he saw Alessandro's face.

"He told me when I was older that Alessandro's hand was wrapped around Stefano's neck. Dad was drunk when he told me. I don't think he remembered the next day. But to my father, Alessandro was the cause of not one, but two deaths, and he never forgot it. He hated Alessandro for it. And all those years growing up, I didn't mind. I used my father's affection against my brother, got everything I wanted. While he was hated, I was loved."

She turns her eyes up to mine.

"I was a brat. I was awful to my brother. And I deserve his hate." Emilia looks down at her lap where she's wringing her hands. She has been since she started telling the story, but I'm not sure she was aware of it. "I could have helped. I could have made a difference with my father, but I didn't." She looks up at me again. "I chose not to."

"You were a child. I doubt your mind calculated that."

"You don't know me."

"I think I do, actually."

She exhales loudly, shakes her head.

"Does Alessandro know where you are now?"

"He didn't."

"Was the whipping all he had planned for you?"

Her eyes study mine for too long before she nods in confirmation. But I know she's leaving something out.

"But now that he knows dad's alive, that he didn't succeed in killing him, he'll look for me. He'll know I was the one hiding him."

"How do you do it? The money, I mean? It must be expensive to hide him, pay for that equipment. I assume he has medical care."

She nods. "He had set up a bank account for me from when I was little. Another perk of being the favorite. I don't know if Alessandro knew about it. I guess not, or he'd have found some way to seize it. He can't anymore. I've moved it. But there isn't a lack of money."

I move back around my desk, have a seat.

I open a folder on my desk, leaf through it, although I've already read its contents. "Your father, his condition is not improving, correct?"

She takes a deep breath in and raises her head so that her chin juts out as she glances at the folder, sees what I'm looking at. She stands, turns the folder over so she can look through it. "Why do you have this? It's my father's medical file."

"I have a right to it, don't you think?"

"No, I don't think you do."

"Well, if I'm responsible for him…"

"You're not responsible for him. You're just helping me keep him hidden for now."

I don't reply.

"Where is he?" she asks, closing the folder. Keeping hold of it.

"Sit down, Emilia."

"Are you going to tell me?"

I scribble an address that's about two hours out of the city on a sheet of paper, hand it to her. "He's here."

From the look on her face, she's surprised I gave her the information. "And Nan too?"

I nod. "Would you like to talk to her?" I offer. "Just to confirm I haven't murdered a dead man."

"He's not dead."

"He's not made any progress in four years. He wouldn't be alive without the machines."

"You don't know that."

"I do, actually. So do the doctors, all of them." Because she didn't stop at a second opinion.

She sits, and her face, it looks like a child's for a moment. I've watched Emilia closely since the beginning. She's controlled to an extreme, she's silent, she's strong, but at the same time, so utterly and completely vulnerable. This is the face of that vulnerability. Like that of a lost little girl. And it makes me fiercely protective.

But the noble, the good, it always has a flip side. A dark intent beneath the facade of good. Because I know I'm not good. And this instinct to protect—along its edges and seeping in at every crack is the desire to claim. The need to own. To possess.

"I want to see him."

"That's not a good idea. The less traffic we have, the better to keep him hidden. But you can call Nan when we're done here."

"Aren't we done?"

"No. There's a meeting tonight. You'll attend with me."

"A meeting?"

"Yes. I have some work to do now. Vincent will take you to your apartment to get what you need. You'll then be brought back here to spend the day. I'd say bring a bikini to swim, but we know how that went last time."

"Fuck you." She stands, takes the file, walks around the chair she just vacated, and puts one hand on the back of it. "I asked for your help with one thing. I asked you to help me keep my father safe. That didn't mean you get to take over my life, every aspect of it. I'm not going to any meeting with you. I'm going to go see my father and then I'm going to go back to my apartment—"

"Where you'll wait for Alessandro?"

At that, she stops. "I can handle myself. I'm stronger than I was when he...did what he did. I'm not the same person anymore."

"You may like to believe that," I check my watch, "but you're still no match for a man."

"It's not what I want to believe. It's the truth."

I stand, ignore her comment, and walk around the desk. I know it takes all she has to remain where she is, hugging her father's medical file to her.

"This isn't up for discussion. You'll be at the meeting tonight, and you'll behave yourself."

"Or what? What if I don't do as you say?"

I cup her ass and squeeze, watch her flinch.

"You really need to ask?" I pause, let my words sink into her thick skull. "Know that I was gentle last night."

"Gentle?" She snorts.

There's a knock on the door. "Come in."

It's Vincent. "Sir, the cars are ready."

"We'll be right there."

He leaves and closes the door. "File," I say, stepping back

and holding out my hand.

"Why do you need it?"

"I don't. I just want it."

"Why?"

"Because."

"I only asked you to keep him safe."

"File."

She exhales, knows she won't win this one. Truly, I could give a fuck about the file, but it's a matter of principle. She hands it over. I thank her, then set it back on my desk.

"Ready?" I ask.

"Why do you want me at this meeting?"

"You're charming company," I deadpan.

"Who's going to be there?"

"Don't concern yourself with that. You'll be with me. You'll be safe."

"Why wouldn't I be safe?" she asks, then stops. "Does whoever it is know that you're bringing me? Emilia Estrella?"

She's been in hiding this long. After tonight, everyone will know she is alive and well. They'll know more than that too, but she doesn't know that just yet, and I don't plan on telling her. No way she'll go along with it if she did.

"No one knows yet."

"But they will."

I study her.

"I don't have a choice, do I?"

"I will keep you safe." I reach out a hand to touch her cheek.

But she slaps that hand away. "You keep saying that, but who's going to keep me safe from you?" She turns, walks out the door and, without another word, is escorted to the car that will take her to her apartment.

13

EMILIA

I'm only allowed twenty minutes in my apartment, and the only moments I get alone are when I close my bathroom door. I'm back at Giovanni's house without delay where the first thing I do is call Nan. She sounds relieved to hear from me and she tells me she and dad are safe. Two doctors have come to look at him, which I have to ask Giovanni about because he doesn't need new doctors, and the only help I asked for was that he keep him safe from Alessandro. She says there are a dozen armed men, and although she'd rather be at home, she feels safer to have them here now that Alessandro knows dad's alive.

I'm given free rein of the house. I have lunch and spend an hour outside trying to flip through a magazine, but my mind is too distracted. I go inside and, after making sure the cook is in the kitchen and none of his men are around, I casually try the study door. It's locked. I guess I knew it would be, but it was worth trying. I try the other doors too, and the only one that is unlocked, apart from his bedroom, which I've already searched, is the one to the library. I enter that darker room and stand looking around at the two stories of books along the walls. The comfortable chairs.

I sit in one of them, the leather worn, the seat swallowing me up, hugging me. I tuck my knees up and let it. I like it in here. It's dark, and I guess it feels safe. And the longer I sit here, the more I think I can feel him in here.

His tumbler is sitting on the table beside the chair, and there's a sip of that burning liquid in it. I pick it up, inhale. Then I put it to my lips and swallow the few drops that are left. I don't know why I do this. I put the glass down and lay my head on the back of the chair.

It's so quiet here. So still. I wonder if he comes in here in the evenings. If this is where he relaxes. If this is his chair. I can almost smell his aftershave lingering among the scent of leather and whiskey and paper.

What is wrong with you?

I give my head a shake, rub my face. I get up, take a turn around the room, pull a book out, read the title, put it back.

After some browsing, I go to the window. It's wrought iron and looks out over the backyard. I check the time, then take another round, this time stopping at the podium-like table against the wall. I turn on the light there, and it illuminates the large world atlas on top of it. It's an old one. I open it, leaf through some of the pages, liking the old maps, the smell of the paper. That's when I come across something strange. Maybe a bookmark, I think, and I turn to the page. It's a map of Italy. Southern Italy, to be precise. I pick up the bookmark. It looks like an old Polaroid. I turn it over and gasp. Because the image I see is of a girl. And I know who she is right away. It's her. His tutor.

And it's not just a slight resemblance we share.

It's the strangest feeling, but this could be a photo of me. Everything, especially the eyes. They have the same shape, that same strange color, although the look inside hers, it's different. So very different than mine.

And I can't help but wonder if that's why he wants me. Is it that I look like her? Is he thinking about her when he's fucking me?

I decide I don't care about that the moment the thought arises. I push that twisted nudge of jealousy aside because I can't be jealous. That's not what I am feeling.

He's the first man I've fucked in a long time. The first man I've chosen to fuck.

Although is that true? I mean, he chose me, right? It's not like I decided. Although I know if I'd said no, he wouldn't have forced me. Like when he punished me last night, I know he was careful. I know he could have been harsher. He could have used his belt. Broken skin. Hell, he could have crippled me if that's what he wanted.

Maybe I'm stupid to think this at all, but I do feel safe, knowing he will protect me. I think maybe he's the only one who can keep me safe against Alessandro. Dad could, once, but not anymore.

Dad.

I shake my head and return my attention to the photo.

Beneath the photo are scribbled dates. She was twenty-three when she died. One year younger than I am now.

A shudder runs through me.

I drag my gaze over to the page beside the one of her photograph. There's a folded, yellowing sheet of paper there. As much as I know it's a violation, I pick it up, unfold it. I know I should put it back the moment I realize that it's a letter from her to Giovanni. But it's in Italian. I double-check the date against the one on her photo. Strange. She wrote it a few days before she died. I can pick out a few words, guess their translation based on my Spanish. I don't get much farther than that, though, because I hear a door close, and I'm startled. Because I'm caught.

How can a man his size be so quiet? How did I not hear the door open?

Giovanni stands in the room. I watch as his eyes fall on the podium, on the open letter. He doesn't say anything. He's carrying a bag, a garment bag, which he sets over the arm of the chair I'd sat in just a little while ago.

I step away when he nears the podium. He picks up the letter, scans it, and I watch him when he folds it, sets it down, and looks at her photograph. I watch his face as his eyes fall on it. But I don't know what I'm looking for, and he's too good at hiding whatever it is he's feeling because I can't read him.

He returns it to the atlas, taking care to put it facedown. He closes the book then turns to me.

"Interesting reading?" he finally asks, his voice level. Like we're talking about the weather.

"It was in Italian, so no." My heart is racing. I don't know how he'll react, but it's not that he forbade me to enter this room. It's not that I broke in, and it's not like I was snooping. It was just there.

Still, when he takes a step toward me, I take one back, but that's a mistake because I've backed myself into a corner.

"Are you afraid of me?"

I don't answer. I don't want to lie, but I won't admit the truth.

He grins. My silence is answer enough. He sets one hand on the wall beside me, leans into it. Into me. His gaze roams over my face then downward.

"Don't you want to ask me anything?"

I shake my head no, but we both know it's not true.

"Come on," he taunts, setting his forearm on the wall,

leaning into it. He undoes the top button on my shirt, then the second, then the third, and slides his hand inside to cup my breast, knead my nipple. My breathing is ragged by the time he pulls his hand out and meets my eyes. "You must have some questions? I told you all you had to do was ask."

I stare up at him, and every hair on my body stands on end as I again shake my head.

He leans in close, so close his nose is almost touching mine. "Ask me your fucking questions."

"I look just like her."

"I already told you that, and that's not a question."

"Did you…is she…did you hurt her?"

"There you go," he says, backing up a little, giving me a dark grin. "No. I didn't hurt her. But I didn't save her either."

I'm processing his words when he continues.

"That letter, I finally found out what my father did. When I understood why she did it. Why she killed herself. Too little too late, though. So no, I didn't hurt her. I hurt him. And this letter is a reminder to me. A reminder that trust is for fools. That family will betray you like no other."

I know this already. I know the sting of blood betrayal.

Abruptly, he steps back, but not far enough that I can slip past. He takes my hand, and his grip is tighter than it needs to be.

"Does that satisfy your curiosity?" He doesn't wait for me to answer but continues. "Let's go upstairs," he says, but I draw back.

"Is that why you're the way you are?"

"And how is that?"

"Cruel." I don't mean it. I don't know why I say it.

He exhales. Cocks his head to the side. "You don't know cruel, Emilia."

"You have no right to say that. You don't know me like you think you do. You don't know what I've been through."

His eyes narrow. "Then tell me. Because I'm dying to know. Because what I'm thinking is that lashing your brother gave you, there's more to it that you're hiding and I can't figure out if you're protecting him or yourself."

But he doesn't give me a chance to respond, and I'm glad because I can't. Not only do I not want to, I can't. Instead, he picks up the bag and, with my hand in his, he walks me up the stairs to the third floor, to his bedroom. There, he releases me.

"Get undressed."

"Why?"

"Because I said so."

I stand there as he unzips the garment bag, takes the dress out. He holds it up to show it to me.

It's beautiful, a dark red that will compliment my olive skin and dark hair. But there's a problem with it.

"I can't wear that."

"Why not?"

"It has no back." It's a halter-top dress, with a deep V down the front and cut on a bias low on the back. It's long, floor-length, but the back is cut so low, it will frame every single mark on my back like a painting.

"That's the point. Get undressed. Put it on. I want to see you in it."

I swallow. It's hard to breathe sometimes when he's close like this.

When I don't move, he tosses the dress on the bed and comes toward me, walking me backward, kissing me just as my back hits the wall. He pulls the shirt I'm wearing over my head and turns me around. He unhooks my bra and peels it off before reaching around to unbutton my shorts. His fingers brush over my mound, my clit, and I suck in a breath. But that's not what he wants right now. He pushes my shorts from me, takes my hands, and places them flat against the wall. My panties are the last to be stripped off. Once I'm naked, he stands back.

He's close, but he's not touching me. I feel him behind me, though. Feel his eyes on me. The heat of his body near mine. I turn my head, so I can see him from the corner of my eye. He takes off his button-down shirt, tosses it on the bed, and steps closer to lift my hair up and set it over my shoulder. His touch is soft. He's not hurting me. He nudges my legs apart with his own and kisses the nape of my neck, and when he steps back, I set my forehead against the wall.

"You're beautiful."

A moment later, I gasp as I feel two fingers dip into my folds, then rub my clit. He pulls them away, and I hear him undo his belt, unzip his pants. His hands cup my ass, splay me open. His breathing is shorter, and so is mine as I anticipate what will happen. What he'll do. And when he slides his thick cock into me, I bite my lip and take him, feel him stretch me.

"Do you want me because I look like her?" I force myself to ask only because I don't have to look at his face when he answers.

He's moving slowly, hands keeping me spread, my pussy wet for him, dripping for him. He pulls out, and I feel a sense of loss. When I move, he sets one hand on top of mine and the other on the back of my head, turning my forehead back into the wall, keeping my arms over my head.

"Stay."

"Do you?" I ask again. He brushes his knuckles over my back, right down the center of it.

I gasp, it's barely a touch. He's being careful with me,

and that featherlight touch is sending shudders along my spine.

His mouth is on me then, kissing the back of my neck. My eyes close, and I catch my breath. I hear how it quivers as he tenderly kisses what must be every ugly scar on my back.

"Do you want me because I remind you of her?" I don't want to ask it. I don't want to spoil this moment, this tenderness, but I have to. Because tenderness, it doesn't belong to me.

My eyes are still closed, and I'm still just feeling him when he reaches my lower back, kisses me there.

"Is that it?" I ask.

He straightens. He's naked behind me and pressing against me. He kisses my cheek. "No," he says before sliding down, splaying me open again, licking the length of me, then coming back up to kiss my cheek.

"Is it because you couldn't save her? Am I your second chance?"

He stops, and I feel his body go rigid, just for a minute, just long enough to tell me there's some truth to my words.

"I was a boy then, Emilia. And she's dead and buried. Let her lie. This isn't about her. I'm here with you. *You*." His fingers slide down over my back again. "I have no secrets. But you? These lines? They hide something. Something darker lies beneath them. Tell me. Tell me your secrets."

But he's kissing me again, my back, my neck. It's not my secrets he wants. Not right now. I wonder if he'd want me at all if he knew. If he'd touch me like this.

A tear runs down my cheek, then another. I feel my hands slipping from the wall, and I'm cold, so cold. He's naked behind me, taking my arms, hugging me to him from behind. He drags my arms upward, takes both wrists into one hand and holds them against the wall as he resumes kissing my neck, my back. He turns me around, and I know he isn't surprised by my tears because he kisses them too. He kisses my face, then my mouth, and it's the most sensual thing I've ever felt. The most erotic touch. The most gentle.

I don't know gentle. I never have. All the men in my life have hurt me. All except my father. I thought Giovanni was just one more to add to that list.

My arms wrap around his shoulders, and I'm kissing him back. My eyes are closed, and I feel the urgency to be with him. It's not the sex. It's not getting off. It's not those things, and it scares the fuck out of me what it is. I wonder if he feels it too. This need. This strange need to be close. Closer. Closest.

A moment later I'm lying beneath him, Giovanni's still kissing me, and when he slides inside me, I catch my breath and barely stop the words that are about to tumble from my mouth because they make no sense. They can't.

I know he feels the shift the moment it happens, the instant I stiffen, because his fist is in my hair and he's forcing my head back, forcing my eyes to open.

"What happened to you?" he asks, but he's still fucking me. Watching me intently as he thrusts.

I shake my head, feel a tear slide from the corner of my eye down over my temple. I hold onto him, hold him tight to me. I don't want to talk. I don't want his eyes on me. I don't want him to see me. I just need him to hold me like this for a little bit. Just for a few minutes because I can't ask for more. Forever doesn't belong to someone like me. I just need to feel him inside me now, feel his weight on me, covering me, hiding me.

Smothering me.

Making me disappear.

"Emilia," he groans.

I know he's close. I squeeze my legs around him and draw him deeper inside me. His thrusts come harder, pushing the breath from me, and when he comes, he bites my neck, burying his face in my hair, and I hold him. I hold him and he can't see me and I am sobbing and I have to stop. He's throbbing inside me, his cum is filling me up. And I wish we could stay like this forever. I wish I could hide here forever. Safe and protected, hidden from the world.

"What the fuck happened to you?" he asks without raising his head from the crook of my neck.

What he says, it makes me turn my head away, makes my heart hurt. Because if he knew how damaged I was, how truly broken, how sick, he wouldn't want me. He wouldn't want to touch me. And he'd be right to run the other way.

He moves, and I force back my tears. His breathing is ragged, and he's warm against me. When he pulls out, I feel his cum slide out, and I wish I could hold it inside me. Hold a little piece of him. Because this is going to slip away. I know. It's coming, the end. And I think when it's over, when it's done, I think I won't be able to put myself back together again. I only just managed it last time. And look at me; I'm like a doll barely stitched together.

Coming apart at the seams.

14

GIOVANNI

I'm standing in my bedroom, listening to Kill's message, my mind and my eye on her. She's in the bathroom putting on makeup, and I can see her reflected in the mirror behind her.

Making love to her just now, it was strange. Different.

Making love. Shit. What am I talking about? What the fuck is wrong with me?

I fuck. I don't make love.

She's wrong about what she said. And it's true what I said. When I first saw her, it was that resemblance that drew me. But she's different. She is so very different than Angelica.

I shake my head but think back to how Emilia clung to me and at the same time, how she used my body as a shield, hid herself from me. And I knew she was crying. The silence of that sobbing, it felt endless, like bottomless grief. I want to know what it is that broke her, because it's not those marks on her back. It's not as simple as that.

Emilia straightens, checking her reflection one final time before coming into the bedroom. I tuck the phone into my pocket and look her over. Her expression is fixed. She gives nothing away. Not a single, goddamned thing.

She's is as unreachable as she is beautiful.

I want more than anything to reach her.

Fuck. I need to get my head out of my ass and in the game because this is fucked up.

I motion for her to turn a circle. She does. For the first time since I've known her, she has her hair loose. I know why, though, and that's not going to work. Not for my purposes tonight.

"Put your hair up."

"Why? I thought you liked it down."

"I do, but you're not doing it to please me."

She cocks her head to the side.

I step to her, push some hair behind her ear, and tilt her face up. "When you ride my cock later, I want it down. For now, I want it up."

Her cheeks flush. She swallows, then collects herself. "I don't understand why you're doing this."

"You just have to trust me."

"You keep saying that. Using that word. But I don't trust you."

"I'm just the lesser of two evils?"

"I hope so."

I shake my head. "Go put your hair up and try not to piss me off."

She presses her lips together but turns to go back into the bathroom. A few minutes later, she emerges with her hair in a bun. It's far from perfect. Pieces are already coming undone. But it'll do.

The dress, on the other hand, is a perfect fit. She's stunning in it. She slips into the high-heeled sandals that go with the dress, and I open the bedroom door.

"I should grab a sweater."

"No need. It'll be warm enough at the club." I don't know that, but I do know if she has anything to cover up her back, she will. And I need the message that gets to Alessandro to leave no doubt in his mind about who the woman I'm with is.

I open the door, gesture for her to go ahead.

She's reluctant, but she does. She's hyperconscious about her exposed back. Vincent is discreet as he leads us to the car, but I have a feeling the men at the club won't be.

"Where are we going?" she asks.

"Mea Culpa."

"What's that?"

"Killian Black's club."

"Why do you want my back bare?"

"Because you have nothing to be ashamed of." It's true. It's just not the reason I'm doing this.

"I'm not ashamed."

"Right."

We arrive. I climb out and help her out. With the flat of my hand on her lower back, I lead her inside. It's noisy, the place is packed. And I'm sure there are spies here. Word will get to Alessandro one way or another that I have his sister. I look at Emilia's face, see her take in the scene. See her look at each of the strippers on their stages, see her surprise at my choice of venue.

"This way," I say, gesturing to the private meeting room at the back. Killian stands just outside with Hugo at his side. They watch us coming, eyes unreadable.

"Gentlemen," I say, shaking Kill's hand first, then Hugo's.

"Giovanni." Killian's eyes slide to Emilia, who is cautiously watching. I don't introduce her.

"They here?"

"Every one of them."

"Give you much trouble?"

"Well, they didn't come willingly, but we didn't think they would, did we."

"And the women?"

"Downstairs."

"Good. Thank you for your trouble. The other matter…" I let my words trail off.

Killian's gaze wanders to Emilia then back to mine. "I have some information and should have more in the next hour. Come upstairs when you're finished. Hugo can watch the girl."

I nod and guess Emilia should be fuming at his referring to her as "the girl," but she's too anxious to notice.

When we reach the door to the meeting room, she abruptly puts her hand on my arm. "Who's in there?"

"Friends of Alessandro."

Her mask of composure slips for just a second, just long enough for me to see that little girl underneath, the glimpse I had one other time. Except this time, she's not lost. She's terrified.

"Please don't make me," she pleads. She's never begged before. Never let herself stoop so low. "Please."

"I told you, you'll be safe. I won't let anyone hurt you."

"You don't understand—"

I turn to her, take her arms, squeeze. "You had every chance to tell me what the hell you're so afraid of. What it is that happened. But you didn't. You wanted to keep your secrets. Thing is, Emilia, my asking, it wasn't ever a request. So, unless you want to talk now…"

She studies me, searches my eyes, then lowers her lashes. I push the door open and step inside, pull her inside with me.

Six men are sitting at the table, two wearing suits, the others in T-shirts and jeans, all looking a little worse for wear. A dozen men stand guard around the room.

I look at each of the seated men, meeting each set of eyes in turn. I memorize the face of the one who has his locked on Emilia. I don't look at her. I don't need to. I know she's staring back at him, the stranger in the dirty T-shirt and ripped jeans, the only one of the six who is leaning back against his seat, his greasy head resting casually against the back of the chair. When he moves his hand to scratch his armpit, I see how dirty his nails are.

But the thing that gets my hackles up isn't any of this. It's the one corner of his mouth that's curved up into a smirk. It's the fact that I feel Emilia tremble beside me. Feel her nudge closer to me, seeking safety. Protection. It's in the small sound she makes that I know she hopes no one hears. That trembling exhale, the fear in the soft breath, the desperation.

"Vincent," I say, not taking my eyes off the man who's looking at her. At every inch of her. I feel my hand tightening around her arm. I know I'm hurting her, but it's not her I want to hurt.

"Sir." Vincent is beside me.

I hand her to him, make sure he's got hold of her because I'm not sure she won't collapse if left to stand on her own.

Once Vincent has her, I step over to the man whose smirk has widened into a grin. I instantly have my fingers in his greasy hair and yank his head back hard. I want to keep pulling. I want to tear his head off his body. Rip him apart.

"You keep looking at her like that, and I'll pop your eyeballs out of their sockets and feed them to you, understand."

It's not a question. I don't want an answer. I slam his face into the table then release him, step back, and adjust the sleeve of my suit jacket.

A quick glance at Emilia shows me her white face. Her eyes have gone huge, and she's trembling, but she's not looking at me. She's still staring at him. Can't take her eyes off him. Doesn't even blink.

And I've never seen her this afraid.

This was a mistake.

Bringing her here was a mistake. I'll fix it, but first, I need to get a message to these men.

"Gentlemen." I use the term very loosely. "In case you don't know who I am, my name is Giovanni Santa Maria."

No one speaks. Two are still staring at the one who's bleeding all over himself.

"You're here because of your continued loyalty to Alessandro Estrella."

"We don't know where he is," one of the men says. "He fucking disappeared like a fucking ghost. Left us to clean up his shit."

"I don't give a fuck what he left you with. That's not my problem. I want Estrella. You're going to smoke him out of whatever hole he's hiding in and bring him to me."

"Where is my wife?" one of the men asks. "They took my wife."

"Mine too."

"Your women are downstairs." I did take them, one from each man. Wife, girlfriend, daughter, I didn't care.

"They're not involved—"

"Again, not my problem. You have seventy-two hours." I turn to Emilia. When her eyes meet mine, what I see inside them, that desperation, that plea—it almost makes me stop. Almost changes my mind.

Almost.

But this is business. And I can't change my mind. That's not how this works. And so I take her from Vincent and turn her around so her back is to the men.

Some of them gasp. The one with the broken nose just glances up.

"After that, I start marking your women up one by one, just like Estrella marked her up."

When two of the men make to stand, the soldiers along the walls move forward, grip their shoulders, and force them back down. I look once more at the man whose nose I broke.

"Let them go, but keep this one," I tell one of the soldiers, then take Emilia by the arm and walk her out the door.

"Who is he to you?" I ask her the moment we're out in the noisy club.

She just stares past me at that door. I'm not sure she hears me right now. She's still shaking, and her eyes have a strange look to them.

I see Kill walking purposefully toward us.

"Who is he to you, Emilia?"

She rubs the heels of her hands against her eyes, and when she pulls them away, they're black with mascara and eyeliner and there's a dark streak of it across her temple.

"Giovanni," Kill says.

I turn to him, and he drags his gaze from Emilia to me. He looks ruffled, the cuff of his shirt is stained red. It's not like him. Killian Black is always in control.

"I have that information."

"I need to get her home."

"It can't wait. Hugo will put her in a room." Hugo appears behind Kill.

Emilia's eyes snap to mine, and I imagine what she's seeing. Three men. Three powerful, dangerous men. And her between us, at our mercy.

"Vincent." He's at my side in an instant. "Take her home." I take Emilia's arms, make her look at me. She doesn't fight. Doesn't put up any resistance at all. I get that same feeling again, that she has learned which battles to fight. Which ones she won't win. That she knows when to roll over. Give up. And I like it less now than I did before. "I'll be home as soon as I can. We'll talk then."

She doesn't reply, just blinks like she doesn't quite see me. Her forehead is furrowed like she's working something out in her head. Some complicated problem.

I hand her to Vincent and walk to the private elevator, which will take us up to Kill's private office.

15

EMILIA

I thought I was farther along than this. I mean, I knew I wasn't over it, but I didn't know it would be like this. Like seeing him, seeing any one of them, that it would take me right back to those nights. To that basement. To that stench, to me lying in it. Me alone with them. With all of them.

I did fight, in the beginning. They were just stronger than me.

Men like that, like my brother, like them, they like it when you fight. They want you to fight. It gets them off.

Giovanni is like them. He's one of those men. Violence, to him, it's like breathing.

He betrayed me tonight, but that's my own fault. I don't know when I started trusting him, but in a way, I guess I did. Lesser of two evils. He said that. I guess that's what I thought too, but it was a mistake.

His words come back to me, his threat to those men. Does he really intend to hurt their women like Alessandro hurt me? Does he really intend to whip them? At least he doesn't know what else they did. What would he do then? Would he do that to those poor women?

No. No, he's not a monster. He's not like that. He wouldn't do *that*. I don't think Giovanni would steal a soul. Steal the life from it.

It takes me a minute to remember where I am when Vincent clears his throat.

I look up at him, look around. We're back at Giovanni's house. In his garage.

"I want to go home," I say, even though I know it's pointless.

"Giovanni wants you here."

I shake my head. "He said home."

"I need you to go into the house now."

I look down at my lap, at my hands. At the seat beside me. "Where's my purse?"

"You didn't bring one."

"Oh."

He clears his throat again. I climb out of the car and walk into the house because I can't leave. He won't let me. Once we're inside, I go into the living room and go behind the bar to look for a bottle of whiskey. He has several. I find the brand I know, the one my father used to drink, and I pull it out to pour myself some.

That's when I see the shiny pistol hidden there, behind the bottles. I touch it, pull it forward. But I leave it alone and take my drink. I drink it down, all of it, forcing myself to swallow, to not choke.

I then take the bottle and the glass and bypass Vincent, who is standing in the hallway, and climb the stairs up to Giovanni's bedroom. There, I pour myself another glass and strip off this stupid dress and put my shorts and shirt back on that I'd worn earlier today.

I go into the bathroom and wash off my makeup. I scrub my face so hard that it feels too dry afterward. I brush out my hair and pull it into a ponytail. It's messy, but I don't care. Back in the bedroom, I pour another glass of whiskey and lie down on the bed. I can smell us on it. I smell sex. I smell him. It makes me want him again.

God, what is wrong with me?

Lesser of two evils, but not really. Evil is still evil.

I force myself to sit up, to stand. Looking around, I find my shoes and slip them on. They're ballet flats. Soft and comfortable. They're more for inside, but they'll do better than the four-inch heels. Reaching into my pocket, I take out that scrap of paper Giovanni gave me and read the address where Nan and my father are, then shove it away and open the drawer in the dresser where I'd found the cash when he'd left me here alone all day. I don't have my purse, my wallet. I don't know where they are, so I have no choice. I only take what I need. Picking up the bottle of whiskey and my glass, I go back downstairs.

I'm quiet. I know Vincent is here somewhere, but I don't see him. With the pretense of replacing the bottle, I reach for the pistol, make sure it's loaded, and slip it into the waistband of my shorts. It's bigger than I'm used to, heavier too, and it feels awkward, but it doesn't matter. My shirt covers it.

Taking my glass, I walk quietly to the French doors that lead to the garden. There's a slight breeze. It rustles the leaves of the trees.

I walk toward the swimming pool, slip off my shoes, and dip one foot in the water. There's movement inside the house. A glance tells me it's Vincent, so I sit at the edge of the pool and let my legs hang in the water. I look down into it, into the deep end. It's where I almost drowned. Where he saved me. Where he said he wouldn't let me go.

And where I'm sitting, this is the spot where Giovanni made love to me.

He mostly fucks me, but sometimes he makes love. I like it when he does, but it's strange. It makes me feel out of control, and at the same time, it feels right. Feels like that's how it should be. Like when a man touches a woman, it shouldn't always be to hurt.

Giovanni doesn't hurt me—no, that's not true. He does hurt me, but because I want him to. Because he makes me come. He was right the other night. I can only come when I'm hurt.

But tonight, he betrayed me, and now, Alessandro knows where I am. He'll come for me. He'll come to finish the job he started. I escaped him once, but that won't happen again. My luck ran out that night four years ago. I used it up when I somehow managed to crawl out of that basement window. When I managed to move at all, to walk, after what they did.

I shake my head, block the memory. Shove it back into its box.

I can't let it out. I won't survive if I do. If I start seeing them again, seeing their faces, feeling the weight of them on me, their sweat, smelling their smells, feeling them inside me...I can't. I'll drown if I do.

I drag one foot out of the pool, listen to the sound of water drip back in, watch the ripples.

There's a weight to water. What would happen if I just slipped in right now? It would take the slightest movement. A shimmy forward, just a shifting of weight. I could be quiet. Not make a splash like last time when he threw me in. I was scared then. Now, I could just slip beneath the surface and let myself float, let the water carry me, engulf me. Feel myself become weightless. I'd close my eyes this time. I don't want to see. I like the sound of it, of water filling my ears.

But I'm afraid it will hurt when I breathe in. Lungs aren't meant to hold water, and I think it will hurt.

And so, because I am a coward, I stand and dry my feet as best as I can in the grass and put on my shoes. I walk to the back of the garden where there's a door. It's locked, I know from the last time, but I take the pistol out of the waistband of my shorts and aim it at the lock, and I fire.

It's loud, and I know Vincent hears, but it doesn't matter because I'm fast. When the door falls open, I run. I run out into the street, and I keep running. I don't look back. I don't look over my shoulder. Not once. I just run and run and run until I'm engulfed not by water but by people. By so many people that I can disappear.

16

GIOVANNI

Kill hands me a glass of whiskey and pours a generous one for himself.

"Hugo got a little more out of John Diaz, which eventually led to some photographs," Kill says once he's finished his glass.

"Photographs?"

He nods.

"You've seen them?"

"Yes. And you should know, it's bad."

I feel every muscle tense. "How bad?" I need to be prepared. I've been unprepared with her once before.

"I don't know the girl, but after seeing what I saw, I hurt that motherfucker. I don't know what kind of deal you made with him, but he's wishing he was dead right about now, and the only reason he's not is because you wanted him kept alive." He points to an envelope lying on the table among several monitors. "I'll leave you to it."

I hear myself thank Kill in a voice like my own but not quite mine. I stand there, holding my drink, not quite drinking, though, and watch as he disappears into the elevator.

His expression is hard, unrelenting as the doors slide closed, and I'm left alone. I turn, set my glass down, and pick up the envelope. I sit behind the desk and open it. And I stare. I just stare at the grainy color photo. I guess it was taken with a phone. Blown up to 8x10. The quality is bad, or the camera was dirty. But not bad enough to hide this.

It takes me a full minute to turn it over and look at the next one. I only do it after I've memorized every face in that first one, recognizing three easily. Emilia, John Diaz, and the asshole whose nose I broke tonight. The rest I don't know. They're in the other photographs as well. Just as I wonder who took the pictures, I see. A selfie. Alessandro and Emilia. Except he's the only one smiling. And I know they're in chronological order. I can see it on her face. I can see exactly when the fight went out of her. I can see when she learned to roll over and survive. Just survive.

The whipping wasn't what broke her.

Five men.

Five pieces of shit.

Five pieces of shit and her brother, the grand master. And lying on the floor between them, one bleeding, broken girl.

Rage churns in my gut. Rage and a burning need to do violence. To hurt. To break. To kill. Slowly. Painfully. To maim. To dismember. And finally, to wipe from the earth.

I stand up. Push the button for the elevator. Get on. Music assaults my ears when the doors slide open. I step out, but it's like I can't hear or see anything.

My hands are fists of concrete and my body is steel. A weapon more deadly than a gun.

Hugo and Kill are waiting for me by the doors that lead to the downstairs rooms. I don't acknowledge the looks on the faces of the people I pass. Of the sea that parts as I approach. I catch a glimpse of myself in a mirror, and I don't recognize myself. My eyes are hard, like stone. Rage has turned them almost black. The tension in my muscles makes me look even bigger.

Neither Kill nor Hugo speak, but they follow me down the steel stairs, the sound of three approaching men like a death sentence because each one of us, we're lethal.

One of the overhead lamps blinks. I keep walking. I know where to go. I know which door the asshole from tonight is behind because at Kill's nod, a soldier opens a door, and I step inside.

He's leaning against the far wall, arms folded across his chest. When he sees me, he straightens, alarm stealing the arrogant assuredness of his expression. His nose has stopped bleeding, but it's about to start again.

"Leave us alone," I say, my voice unfamiliar. Like that of someone caged and seething for too long. Like some rabid animal.

The door closes behind me, and I'm alone with him. He's putting his hands up, and I think he's trying to say something, but I don't hear him. I can't. Rage is ringing too loud for me to hear anything but it.

I move directly to him, take his hair into my fist, and this time, it's the wall I smash his head against, and it's not just once. This time, I don't stop. I do it again and again and again. Blood is splattering against my face, in my nose, my eyes. It's in my mouth, but I still don't stop.

He's gone limp, and his face, it's collapsing...collapsed. He no longer looks human, and there's so much blood, but I only realize it when I drop him. When I see the pool I'm standing in, that's stained my shoes and ruined my suit.

But I still don't stop.

He's dead. Long dead. But I kick his gut, his back, his

broken face. I beat him until every bone in his body is broken and only regret I didn't start with this. I didn't start with the pain before killing the piece of shit.

When I'm done, I wipe the back of my hand across my face, my nose, but it only smears the blood, doesn't wipe it away. I don't feel anything when I look at the man on the floor. When I look at the mess I've made. I don't feel good or bad or less human. And I don't feel satisfied either.

One bang of my fist against the door, and it opens. Kill and Hugo are outside. They glance into the room when I make my way to the door behind which John Diaz is waiting to die.

The guard opens that door, and I step inside to find him drinking water through a straw. He's sitting in his stupid fold-out chair, drinking his last water. When he sees me, he stumbles to his feet, knocking the chair down behind him. He drops the bottle, spilling the water, and falls backward.

I won't make the same mistake with him. I'll do it differently. Opposite. Slow. Although I can't promise too slow.

One word keeps repeating in my head. One single word.

Rapist.

He mutters something as I pick him up, but he can't talk because half his tongue is missing, and I slam my fist across his jaw and send him flying into the wall, and I don't stop. I don't stop until he, too, is a pulp of blood and guts and death.

17

EMILIA

He's gone.
He's gone. No one is here. Nan. My father. The soldiers. No one.

The taxi is waiting a block away, and I think I should go back before he leaves. He's already been paid. He can take off and abandon me here.

We're a couple of hours outside the city in a town I've never heard of. It's the opposite of the city—small and quaint and quiet. The address is a simple house in a normal neighborhood, and the only sign there was anyone here recently is that there are two empty bottles of beer in the sink and a half-eaten container of takeout that doesn't yet stink in the fridge.

There are two floors with one bedroom downstairs and two more upstairs. I know he was here, my father. Or someone was who had to be wheeled in and out. I can see the tracks on the floor. What happened, though? Who moved him? If Alessandro found him, he'd be dead. I'd have found a bloody massacre if my brother had found him, so that's not it. Did Giovanni move him? Why? Why would he? It makes no sense.

Or did he give me a false address, knowing I'd come?

I'm angry, but anger is good. It's better than fear. To be afraid is to be weak.

I open the kitchen door and step into the backyard. It's big and nestled between tall trees, a whole forest. It's so dark here, I can see stars. I almost never see stars. I look up at them, listen to the silence. Silence does have a sound. Heavy, like water. It can be deafening. The noise of the city, I need it. This utter stillness, it would kill me.

It's cooler up here than in the city. I hug my arms to myself, wishing I had a jacket or better shoes. I go back inside to take one more turn through the house before leaving, but when I'm in the kitchen, I hear a car pull up outside. Hear two doors open and close. I take my gun out of the waistband of my shorts and listen to the approaching footsteps. Men, I can tell. It's always men. Their footfalls are heavy. I wish I could see from here, but the kitchen window overlooks the backyard. Whoever it is is coming up to the front door.

My heart is racing as I hear the door open. Am I expecting Alessandro? And what will I do if I see him? Shoot? Can I? Am I strong enough?

But I don't have to think about that because at the same time the front door opens, so does the kitchen door, and I'm taken by surprise. I shift my gun from the man at the front to the one behind me, just processing Giovanni's outline as I pull the trigger, the sound crashing through the clean, clear night. Tainting it.

Simultaneously I'm thrown against the wall, and my head hurts with the impact, disorienting me. He uses that instant to disarm me, catching me as I begin to fall forward.

The lights go on, and it's too bright. Too artificial.

"What the fuck is it with you and guns?" Giovanni asks, keeping hold of me as he checks the chamber of the pistol, engages the safety, and tosses it to Vincent, who catches it.

"Let me go!"

"I feel like we're on repeat sometimes, you and me."

"What are you doing here?" I ask, struggling for him to free me. He's got me cradled against him and has both my wrists in one of his hands.

"I got this, Vincent. Wait outside for us."

Giovanni turns his full attention to me. I hear the front door close and stare up at him. He's taken off his jacket, and his shirt sleeves are rolled up. There's blood on his clothes, but I don't think it's his. But it's not his clothes I'm interested in. It's the way he's looking at me. It's different. There's something different in his gaze.

It takes him a full minute to let me go. I step back when he does, rubbing my wrists.

"Where's my father?"

"I moved him this afternoon. This was just a temporary location."

"Where did you move him to?"

"Why? You going to run off to the next house?"

"I have a right to know."

"Why did you leave the house? I put you there for your own safety."

"I can take care of myself. I don't need you. And I don't want you. Just leave me alone." I take a step, wanting to get around him. But he stops me.

"Where are you going?"

"I have a taxi waiting."

"No, you don't."

"I do, he's around the block."

"I sent him on his way. You'll go home with me when I'm ready."

I take a step back, feel the sadness of earlier creeping back in. Feel that hopelessness. "Why? I don't know what else you want with me. I mean, tonight, you set me up. You act like you're putting me in that dress for me, telling me I have nothing to be ashamed of—"

"You don't. What happened wasn't your fault."

I stop for a second. It's his tone as much as what he says. It's like he means so much more than he should mean. Than he should know.

But I don't want to think about that, so I go on. "You betrayed me. You put me on display. You used me and humiliated me when I trusted you."

"You don't trust me. You never did. You said so yourself."

"And, God," I shake my head. "Would you really do what he did to me to someone?" I ask, thinking about the women he threatened to have whipped.

"Emilia—"

"Would you?"

"Let's go home, Emilia." He takes my arm.

I tug it free. "My home is separate from yours, and I have to find a new one now."

"I told you, I'm not going to let your brother hurt you."

"You can't keep me safe forever. He'll come for me. I got away once. I'm not getting away again. You think I don't know that?"

He looks at me strangely, almost sadly. He touches my face, my cheek.

"I know what those men did to you."

My brain processes his words in slow motion. Like his speech is slowed down on a recording or something. And no, it's not sad, that look. I'm wrong. It's pity. It's pity I see in his eyes. I think about what happened before I left. Think about how that man, Kill, wanted to talk to him alone. Remember how he was looking at me. But there's no way they know anything. It's not possible.

"Did you hear me?" he asks.

I slap his hand away and back up, hug my arms to myself. "Get away from me."

He comes closer to me. "Emilia, look at me."

I didn't realize I wasn't, but I just look up at his chest. I can't look at his eyes, not if he knows.

It's colder in here suddenly, and I'm shivering.

Giovanni's hands close gently over my arms, then he begins to rub them.

I shake my head, back up some more, hit the wall.

"I killed two of them. The one you saw tonight and Diaz. They're dead."

I shift my eyes slowly up to his. I saw him break that man's nose. Heard what he said about popping out his eyeballs and feeding them to him if he continued to look at me. Apart from my father, no one has ever defended me before.

But that doesn't mean anything. Not a single thing.

"They didn't do anything to me." My voice breaks.

"I saw the pictures, Emilia."

God. Pictures. Alessandro took pictures. I had forgotten that.

But I shake my head.

"I need the names of the others. It'll help to find them faster. Do you know them? Know their names?"

The floor is linoleum. It's an ugly, dirty green. It must be as old as the house.

"Emilia. Are you listening to me?"

I look up at him, and he's a little blurry at first, but I

swallow back my tears. Swallow what I can around the lump in my throat.

"Do you know I came?" I say.

"What?"

"I came. When they fucked me. I came."

God, I'm going to be sick. I turn to the sink, dash to it, grip the cold edge, but it's just a dry heave. I don't know when I last ate. I stand there and hug my belly and my hair's falling out of its ponytail and hanging in the sink and I shove it back. Shove it in place. But it won't stay away.

"Emilia." He's pulling me back, turning me to face him, but I don't want to see him. I don't want him to see me.

"I came every time. With all of them."

He finally succeeds in turning me around, makes me look up at him, and I feel tears and snot on my face. It's gross. But he's just looking at me like he doesn't care about that.

"Come here," he says, pulling a paper towel from the rack that's hanging on the wall and wetting it before cleaning my face.

"And then, when they were done, or when I thought they were done, they hung me from the ceiling and laughed and got hard all over again while Alessandro opened up my back." Rage is nudging some of that hopelessness out of the way. But still, that feeling of nausea, of wanting to puke, to get everything out, it makes me clutch my belly, cover my mouth. "And then...then..."

"We don't have to do this right now."

"No, you should hear. You should know everything." I shove away from him, wipe the backs of my hands across my face because it's wet again. "It's what you want, right? I mean, pictures can't tell the whole story. I can, though. I was there for the whole thing. Guest of honor, I guess."

"Let's go home." He reaches for me.

I shake my head, slip away into the living room. "After. After, they did it again. They each had a turn again. I was still strung up. I could stand on tiptoe at first, but then I couldn't anymore. I couldn't get a grip. Everything hurt too much." I look down at the floor, at my pretty shoes so out of place here. Note the ugly brown carpet. I bet it's rough to the touch. And full of germs. "I had their cum inside me. Their disgusting cum. I can feel it sometimes, you know? Feel them. It makes me sick."

"That's enough."

I shake my head, because it's not enough. It will never be enough.

I climb up the stairs. They have that same carpet on them. I didn't notice it earlier. I didn't notice any of it. The bedrooms up there have been closed up so long they smell.

"Come here, Emilia. We're leaving."

"Why don't you leave me alone?" I go into the bedroom with a mattress on the floor. It's gross, stained and filthy, but I need to lie down, and I don't care anymore. There is too much dirt. I can't do anything about it anymore. "Why don't you go away." I try to close the door, but he doesn't let me.

"I'm not leaving you alone. And certainly not here."

I stop. A strange laugh comes from my mouth. Like a sound a crazy person would make.

"Emilia, come here. I'm not going to tell you again."

"They need to open the windows. It's too dank in here." I shove at one. It doesn't give at first, so I shove harder. It goes flying up, and I stumble, catching myself on the sill. The wood is rotting, and a splinter buries itself in the center of my palm.

"Emilia! Get away from the fucking window!"

That laugh is there again. I don't understand why he's

still here, and I don't really know why I'm leaning so far out. It's only two stories. It's not a bad fall. Not even close. I probably wouldn't even break a leg.

"Jesus Christ!"

His hand around my arm is like a vice. It hurts when he tugs me back, the wood scratching my hands. I crash into his chest. He catches me, but when I look up at him, he's nothing but mad. He gives me a hard shake.

"What the fuck do you think you're doing?"

I shove at him, shove at his chest. Because I'm mad too.

He shakes his head and, with just a nudge against my chest, he shoves me against the wall.

"Don't roll over. Don't fucking give up!" he yells at me. "You fight. You get fucking mad. You hit someone. Hit me."

I do, I slap my hands against his chest. I know not to slap his face. I make fists and pound him with them.

"Good. Harder. Hit me harder."

"So you'll hit me back?"

"I told you, I don't hit women."

"You did."

"That's a spanking you earned, Sunshine."

"Don't call me that."

"It wasn't ever meant to harm you. Not like what they did."

He kisses me, smashes me against the wall, his lips pressing against mine. His body smothering mine.

"Hit me again. Fight me. Get fucking angry, but don't fucking roll over. That's not you. Not even close."

I grip the sides of his head, pull his hair, let out a wicked, animal like roar as I wrap my legs around his middle. He's kissing me and telling me that's it. To keep going. To keep fighting.

He drops me on the mattress. It's hard, and the springs

dig into my back, but I don't care. I'm tearing at his shirt, and he's already ripped my shirt open, is taking one breast out of the bra while his other hand rips my shorts and shoves them off. He kisses me as I undo his belt, his pants, slide my hand in to cup his cock, his balls. I want him. I want him inside me. Now. I need him now.

He gets up on his knees and shoves his pants down just far enough to free his cock. He shoves my knees wide, holds them spread open, and looks down at me, at my dripping pussy. Pushing my legs down to the mattress, he thrusts deep and hard inside me. I suck in a breath and fist my hands. It hurts, but it hurts so fucking good. Our eyes are locked. He thrusts twice more before pulling out.

I look at him, and he grins at my disappointment. A moment later, he's at my other entrance and, his cock wet with my juices, he penetrates that tight ring. I close my eyes and arch my back. Fuck, I'm going to come so hard.

"Look at me, baby."

Baby. I like that. I like it so much. And I do. I look up at him as he fucks my ass, each thrust deeper, my body stretching to accommodate him, wanting him. When he's fully seated, he lets go of my legs and leans in close enough to kiss me.

"Come for me, baby."

I do. It's like my body wants to please him. He moans as my walls throb around him, and I feel him thickening inside me as he moves. Barely a moment later, we're coming together, and I'm watching his beautiful face and he's so close, so close. We collapse together on that gross mattress, and when he's holding me, I feel myself go limp. I feel myself soften, and for the first time in a very long time, maybe in forever, I let myself go. I relax and my eyes flutter closed. I can smell him, his aftershave, and he feels safe. I curl my face into his chest as he slides out of me and wraps his arms around me. I don't know what happens after that because I fall asleep. It's like all this time, all this running, catches up with me, and I can't stay awake another minute, not one more second. Right away, I'm dreaming. He's holding me, and I'm safe in his arms. And I can't be without him anymore.

Because I think I love him.

18

GIOVANNI

"*I love you.*"

I know she's asleep when she says it, but still, those words jar me.

She doesn't wake when I carry her out of the house, or on the long drive back to the city, not even when I carry her up the stairs and lay her in my bed.

I strip off my clothes, dropping them on the floor as I make my way into the bathroom and switch on the shower. I can still pick dried blood off me, and the knuckles of my right hand are bruised. They hurt, but that's okay. It's good to remember. And I'm not done yet.

I switch off the shower and reach for a towel to dry off. My work isn't done yet. I won't be sleeping tonight.

Two men are dead. Four more have to die. The three who raped her. And the one behind it all: her brother.

Four more men I'll beat to death with my fists.

I put on a pair of jeans, make sure she's still out, and go downstairs to my office. The house is dark, not a single light is on, but I like it this way.

I haven't been this angry in so long. Hell, I'm not sure

I've ever been this angry. Well, that's not true. I was angry when I discovered my father's deception. When I found the letter he'd hidden from me. The one Emilia found in the old Atlas in the library. If I'd received it in time, things would have been different. At least for Angelica.

But I push those thoughts away. There's work to be done.

Sitting behind my desk, I lay out the photos again. All of them. I take a permanent marker out of my desk drawer and put a big red X over the faces of the two dead men. I do this in each of the photos they're in. I pick up the one where they're stringing her up by her wrists. Watch them as they pull the chains over a beam until her toes barely touch ground. She's naked, and there's already blood and cum between her legs. They've already raped her. All of them. All but Alessandro.

I want to know who took the photos of the whipping. It's neither of the two I killed. They're in the shot.

Her back is still unmarked in this one, and from the corner of the shot, I see Alessandro's arm, his angry grip on the whip. Twenty-one lines. I wonder if there's a significance to the number, or if his arm tired or if he just ran out of skin.

The blood from her open back stains them when they rape her again afterward. They don't seem to care. I wonder if they were stoned because, even given who I am, what I've done, it's inhuman what they do to her.

But I have to look at these differently. Block any emotion. Anything human. And I can't ever let her see them.

I collect the photos and lock all but one in one of the desk drawers. The one I keep, it has all their faces in it. The two dead men. The four with their days numbered. Her.

I boot up my laptop. As I wait for it to load, the study door opens, and Emilia is standing there. My mind immediately wanders to earlier tonight. To her whispered words. I wonder if she remembers.

"You can't hurt those women."

It takes me a second to understand what she's talking about. The women I threatened to have marked up like she's been marked up.

"Don't worry about that right now."

She steps inside without waiting for an invitation. "I mean it. You can't do this to them. You don't understand what it'll do to them."

"I'm not going to have them raped." I realize my mistake the instant the word is out because she flinches, like I've slapped her. I get up to go to her, but she straightens, steels her spine.

"What are you doing?" she asks.

I'm glad I put the photographs away. "Nothing. Why don't you go back to bed. It's late."

"I'm not tired."

I can't read her. She's closed herself off again. I don't know why that bothers me. "I thought you'd be exhausted."

"You mean after my breakdown?" She walks inside and comes over to the desk.

I turn the photo over.

"What's that?"

"Nothing."

"Is it one of the photographs?" She's a different person to the one she was a few hours ago.

"Go back to bed, Emilia."

She raises her gaze to mine. "No, Giovanni." She reaches out for the picture, but I put my hand over hers.

"You don't have to do this."

"Do what?"

"You don't have to see them."'

"How many are there?"

"Enough."

"Your clothes were bloody," she says, shifting gears. "Upstairs, I mean. From tonight."

She touches the back of my hand, the one that's resting on the image. She lifts it up, holds it between hers, and traces the swollen knuckles, the cut skin. She then pushes it out of the way, and I let her. I watch her turn the photograph over, and I study her when she does, when she looks at the image. And for the smallest millisecond, emotion flashes through her eyes. For that uncountable sliver of time, she's vulnerable again. She's that broken girl on the floor.

She moves her hand, and with her pointer finger, she traces the two X's. She's pressing hard on the photo because it moves in the line she makes. When she's done with those, she points to one of the men. Says a name. She does the same with the other three I don't know. I don't have to write them down. I memorize them. I won't ever forget them.

But then she starts to rattle off other names, facts, birthdays, and finally addresses.

"What are you doing?" I ask.

She has her finger over her own face in the photograph like she's blotting it out. She looks up at me.

"Names and addresses. You said you wanted those."

"You've known all along?" They're all in the city. All but one, who is in New Jersey, but all are close. Too close.

"I don't ever plan on being taken by surprise again."

"Why did you decide to stay in the city?"

"I grew up in this city. Where else should I have gone?"

Anywhere, I think. But I don't say it. "I'll pick up these men within the day."

She nods. "Can I see them when you do?"

"Why do you want that?"

"Because I didn't expect it to be like it was when I saw the one tonight. I thought I was farther along. Not over it—I don't know if that will ever happen—but I didn't think he'd have the effect on me that he did."

"And what makes you think it won't be the same with the others?"

"I'm ready now. Prepared."

"I'm not sure that's a good idea."

"Because it fucked me up? Made me crazy?"

"Why are you doing this to yourself?"

"What, do you care now? Am I some sort of pity project now?"

"I don't pity you. Far from it." I stand up, take her jaw in my hand, and tilt her head upward. "I think you need someone to take care of you right now, that's all."

"And you're that guy?" She snorts, pulls free. "I'm fine, Giovanni. I don't need you to take care of me."

"That's not true. You and I both know it. Go upstairs, and go back to bed like a good little girl now." I sit back down and turn my attention to my laptop. From my periphery, I see her clench her hands.

"I'm not a little girl. Where are the rest of the photos? Who else has seen them?"

I finish reading what's on my screen before turning to her. "Don't worry about that. Do as you're told."

I watch her anger grow, feel it coming off her. She shoves at me and pulls a drawer open, then another.

I close my hand over hers. "Stop. It's enough."

She tugs it away, tries to pull the next drawer open, but this is one is locked.

I'm on my feet in an instant. I capture her wrists, hold them at her back. She tilts her face up. I'm a good head taller than her.

"Anger is good, rage is better, but only if you can control it. If you can't, then it controls you."

She pulls against me, but I don't let her go. She doesn't struggle for long, though. "I don't want to be weak again."

I understand that, but she's got it wrong. "You weren't weak. They were the weak ones. Raping a woman doesn't make you powerful. The opposite."

"What about what I told you?"

"Which part?"

She can't hold my gaze when she says it. "The fact that I came." Her voice breaks, and I know this part is killing her. "What does that say?"

"It says you're human." I soften my grip, slide my hands over hers, and intertwine our fingers. "Don't fucking kill yourself over this. It's done. What they did happened. But it's over. You survived, and they're going to get what's coming to them. That's all you need to remember."

19

EMILIA

I convince Giovanni to let me go to work the next night. He can't keep me locked up inside this house forever. Besides, the Ragoni engagement party is tonight. I have to be there. He has three men stationed on the property, one in the lobby, one in the front lot, and another around the back entrance. Giovanni will be here at midnight to pick me up.

It's a formal engagement party, so I'm dressed in a long lavender gown. It's cut in a deep V down the front, but my back is covered to my neck. I'm in the bathroom off the lobby arranging my hair in a French twist and decide to leave some wisps to frame my face. I like how it looks. It's less severe, much softer than I usually wear it. I tell myself I'll go back to the tight bun on Monday.

Giovanni didn't mention anything about the other night. About what I dreamed I said. I am grateful it was a dream. I don't love him. It's ridiculous to fall in love with the first man who doesn't violate you.

I stop. Shake my head.

If that's my criteria these days, then I am truly pathetic.

After applying a layer of lip gloss, I close my clutch and return to the reception room to see about the setup. The party is beginning to trickle in, and I want to be sure everything is perfect—the flowers arranged, the candles lit, everyone seated before the happy couple arrives. I like engagements, although weddings are my favorite. Most everyone is happy, and it's like it gives me hope. Not for my own wedding. I don't want that. I'm not looking for that. Hope, instead, that it is possible to be happy. I stand and watch everyone for a little while, and I feel the smile on my face. I feel lighter somehow. I know things are far from over with my brother, but it's like having someone know what happened, having someone tell you you're not fucked-up—that you're just human—it somehow lifted the burden, at least a little. I never realized how dark or heavy it was before, I guess.

It's eleven at night when I return to my office. I glance at the front desk, which is empty, since it's shift change. The hotel is creepy when it's so quiet, and it is quiet because the reception hall is in the new addition to ensure overnight guests aren't disturbed. I just have to wrap up a few details before I can leave. I'll go to his house tonight. I'm not sure how I feel about that—or how I should feel, because as much as I miss my apartment, I don't want to be alone. It's like I've been alone for so damn long that my life is just filled with empty space.

But I'm also more anxious now than ever about Alessandro. I know he's going to turn up. And he's got everything to lose with Giovanni as an enemy.

By now, he must know that John Diaz failed in his task to kill our father. He must also know that I am here, within reach. And on Giovanni Santa Maria's arm.

I have to be careful with romanticizing whatever it is

that's going on between me and Giovanni, though. We're not a couple. We won't be one when this is over, either. I have to remember that.

This is what I'm thinking about when I hear the glass door of the sales office open. My desk is around the corner in the open floor plan, where the only person with a private office is the general manager. His door I can see, but the door into the main office I can't.

"Em?"

I hear a woman's voice and realize my heart is pounding. I'm half up from my seat.

"Are you back here?"

"Yes, here," I call out, relieved. It's Lori, one of the front desk staff.

"There you are," she says. I see the wheels of the chair before I see her. See expensive Italian shoes.

My heart races, and I'm half-standing when she comes into view.

"Mr. Santa Maria was looking for you." She is oblivious to my state of mind. She just keeps talking. "And you know how heavy some of the doors are." She gives me a look. The hotel isn't quite in compliance for people with disabilities just yet.

"Oh," I'm looking at the old man and hearing Giovanni's words. His threat to him.

"Well, I need to go. My ride is waiting. You can help Mr. Santa Maria back to the lobby when you're done, right? His driver is waiting outside."

What is he doing here? What does he want with me?

"Em?" Lori asks, confused by my silence.

He just sits there watching me, studying me in that way Giovanni does, but different.

I drag my gaze from his. "Of course." I force the smile I

use at work.

The old man turns his head to look at Lori. "I'm so sorry for all the trouble, dear."

She waves it away. "It's no trouble at all, Mr. Santa Maria. I'm just glad Em's still here."

"Me too," he says, turning his attention back to me.

"Well, goodnight everyone," Lori says.

"Good night," Mr. Santa Maria says, his smile wide, his teeth white and sharp, and his eyes locked on me like he won't look away, not for the world. And I know why that is. Angelica. "Remarkable," he says as soon as we hear the whoosh of the door, letting us know we're alone.

"What are you doing here?"

He wheels himself forward, and I have a feeling he's not as feeble as he led Lori to believe. And when he stops at the space where two desks are too close together to accommodate his wheelchair, he rises to his feet, taking the cane I now notice is attached to the side of the chair.

I was under the impression he couldn't walk at all.

He comes to stand just two feet from me around the side of my desk. Not even. "You really do look like her. Angelica. She has…had…some Mexican roots. That must account for the spectacular beauty." He smiles, bows his head. "I'm sorry. I seem to have startled you. It wasn't my intention. Doubtless our initial meeting has left you with questions and, perhaps, distrust of an old man." He extends his hand to me.

I give a shake of my head. He's an old man. A crippled old man. I don't know what happened between him, Giovanni, and Angelica. I only know that little bit about the affair. Affairs. Giovanni said so himself. He told me there's more to the story. But that doesn't explain the uneasy feeling I have.

"Of course not." I go to him, and I don't like how his eyes run over the length of me. Although hesitating, I place my hand in his. "It's nice to meet you," I say politely.

His grip is remarkably strong. Much stronger than I expect.

"You're a little taller than Angelica was. Poor child."

Child? Strange he should refer to her as a child if he had an affair with her.

He bows a little and brings my hand to his mouth to kiss it. A chill runs up my spine at the contact.

"Mr. Santa Maria, what are you doing here? Giovanni—"

"I sent a note, but I'm afraid it was intercepted. Given what happened at the church, I thought I'd better come."

"A note?"

"Yes, a few days ago. Introducing myself."

He must see from my expression that I never received it.

"Well, I'm not surprised. I know my son well." He looks over at the sitting area and clears his throat.

"Oh. I'm sorry. You'd probably be more comfortable here. Let me help you."

"You're very sweet, dear."

I don't know exactly how to help, though. He's a big man, as tall as Giovanni, at least he was once, but he's more stooped now. He's not as muscular. That's probably due to him sitting in a wheelchair most of the day, but he's still very strong. With his cane in one hand, he wraps his other arm around my waist. It's strange, but I feel rude to pull away. We walk together to the sofa, and I help him sit down.

"Would you like something to drink?" I don't know how I'm being so cordial. Alarm bells are ringing in my head, both for myself and for him. Giovanni's words keep repeating on the heels of those warnings.

"If you have some whiskey, I wouldn't mind it."

"Of course, I'll be right back." I slip away, grateful for the few moments I'll have. I'm unsure what to do. If I should call Giovanni. If I should call security. But I do none of those things. Instead I pour him a whiskey and return to the office. He doesn't see me come back right away, and I have a moment to study him. His expression is fixed and hard and different than it was when we were talking or when Lori was there. Different even than it was at the church. Like those faces are the ones he puts on when someone is watching.

An instant later, he shifts his gaze to mine, and I wonder if I am naive. If he knew I was there all along. But I school my features into a smile. He's not dangerous, I tell myself. He is just an old man. He won't hurt me. Why would he?

I go to him. "Here you are," I say, taking the seat across from him.

"Thank you, dear." He takes a long sip and nods in satisfaction.

"What can I do for you, Mr. Santa Maria?"

"Well, it's more what I can do for you," he says. I'm about to ask what he means when I hear the *swoosh* of the door to the sales office open. I turn to find a man walking inside. Immediately, I'm on my feet, my mouth opening to say something, my heart pounding.

"It's all right, dear," the old man says, and I realize I've backed up to where I'm close enough that he can touch me. His old, cold hand is on my hand. "He won't hurt you."

"What is this about?" I recognize this man. He's the one with whom Giovanni had words in the parking lot.

"Sit down," Mr. Santa Maria says to me. It's not a request. In fact, there's a hardness in his tone.

I look from the old man to the other one, the very capable one.

"Robert, don't stand there scaring the girl. Go get her a

drink," he snaps. If I had any doubt that he wasn't a very capable man, it's now wiped away. He is in charge. In command. The old man facade, it's just that, a facade.

He pats my hand, and I turn to look at him. He smiles, gestures for me to sit beside him.

I do because I don't know what else to do.

"What do you want?" I ask him. Where is Giovanni? Where's the guard Giovanni placed in the lobby?

Robert comes back from the same place I'd just been and hands me a whiskey. I take it, drink a sip.

"That's a good girl."

"What do you want?" I ask again, my voice more forceful.

"Honestly, I just wanted to see you," he says, cocking his head to the side, studying me. "Because when I heard about you, I couldn't really believe it. You do remind me so of Angelica. I wonder what my son thinks he's doing with you. Reliving the past, perhaps?"

I don't know why that bothers me. Maybe because it's been on the back of my mind too?

"Oh, that letter I sent. Here," he reaches into his pocket, takes out a crumpled note.

I take it, open it, read the contents.

Dearest Emilia,

Ghosts we think we killed and buried always lurk nearby, ready to snatch us back in time. Ready to smother us in darkness.

Do not trust my son. He will hurt you like he hurt her.

Be safe.

Your friend,

A.

"I don't understand."

"Robert," Mr. Santa Maria says.

Robert walks to the empty wheelchair, and I realize

there's a bag hanging from the back of it. He unzips it and takes out a large, heavy book. From here I can see it's hand bound.

Mr. Santa Maria takes the book from Robert. I see that both front and back covers are made of carved wood. He takes a quiet minute to look at it, traces the intricate pattern of the carving, then looks up at me. He holds it out.

"I wanted to give this to you. I think you should see it for yourself, because I am quite certain my son has not been fully forthcoming."

My heartrate slows a little as I take the book. It's heavier than I expect, and there's a sick sense of something in my belly. Whatever is inside here, it's not good.

"Go on," urges the old man.

There's a little resistance as I open the book, and I realize it's not really a book but an album or a very expensive scrapbook. No, not that. What's inside doesn't look like happy memories. The opposite. It's a reckoning of sorts. A record keeping.

"Do you read Italian? I thought maybe with the Spanish background?"

I shake my head no, but I can make out the headlines of the newspaper clippings inside. The quality isn't great. I'm guessing the clippings have degraded over time. There are several articles from different papers. Headlines in bold letters. Large photographs. Smaller text that's too hard for me to read. But I guess I don't need to read more than the headlines to understand.

He looks younger, Giovanni. It's just a few years, but there's a difference. I know it's not youth that makes him look so different. It's something else, and that *thing*, whatever it is, there's no longer place for it on his face. On his person.

In one photo he's surrounded by countless people, and he's walking away. Or being led away. He's looking over his shoulder, though, so I can see his face. In his eyes I see a hardness, like the beginnings of what I sometimes glimpse now. What time has turned into a ruthlessness.

"Love triangle, they called it," Mr. Santa Maria says.

I glance at him, and he smiles ruefully as he turns the pages for me until we come to another image. One of Angelica. A different one than the one I saw in Giovanni's library.

He touches the picture tenderly, almost like he's touching her face. He then meets my eyes.

"I understand Giovanni thought he was in love. He was a child, after all, but Angelica," he shakes his head, looks back down at her pictures. "She was mine. Always."

"What about your wife?" I ask stupidly.

His face has lost any tenderness when he looks at me. "Our love died a long time before Angelica entered our lives. It's something my son refused to understand then. Refuses to accept now."

He turns back to the first page, and I look at the photo again. Giovanni in handcuffs. Four policemen are close by, and more stand around, holding the crowd back. Mr. Santa Maria looks me square in the eye when he tells me the next part.

"He hurt her when she told him. When she told him she didn't love him. That she loved me."

"Hurt her?"

He watches me for a long moment, and I think I understand his meaning. I know I do. But he's biding his time. Drawing out the horror. "He raped her, my dear. Violently. She became pregnant, and he insisted she terminate. She couldn't stand up to him. Giovanni will always get his way, no matter how hard he has to push, no matter who he has to hurt."

Ice sweeps through my veins. I stiffen, as if I've turned to stone.

"No, I didn't think he'd tell you that part."

I look down at the image again. I don't know the word for rape in Italian.

"I don't understand," I say, my face buried in the book.

"She committed suicide after that. She couldn't live with herself, live with the violation, the murder of her unborn child. And then he came after me. These stories, the pictures, the papers love this sort of drama, don't they? Family torn apart, father and son at each other's throats, a beautiful, innocent girl the one left hurt—tragically—between them."

I shake my head, close the book, and shove it toward him. "I don't believe it. He wouldn't. He wouldn't do *that*."

He puts it calmly back into my lap. "Keep it. Read it for yourself. You don't have to take my word for it. See in here. In history. Robert," he calls out. The man comes, helps him to his feet. Helps him into his wheelchair. "And when you have finished reading it, you can come to me. I imagine you may not feel very safe in Giovanni's *protection*."

I remain sitting there, looking at the carving on the wood, thinking about his words, and in particular, that last word.

"Take care with that book, Emilia. Keep it hidden from my son. And, more importantly, take care he doesn't do to you what he did to her."

I look up at him, and his gaze doesn't release mine for a long time. Not until he nods, and Robert wheels him out of the office and I'm alone again. Alone with the book that sits as heavy as a brick on my lap.

20

GIOVANNI

Picking up the men who raped Emilia wasn't hard. They weren't expecting me and had all but forgotten the event of four years ago. They remember now, though. Clear as day.

Emilia is waiting for me in her office when I arrive. She startles when I enter and looks paler than usual, but then she smiles. Although I feel like she's forcing it.

"I'm sorry I'm late." I had to go home, shower, and change my clothes before coming here. I don't want her to know the details of the night. "Things took longer than I expected."

"Do you have them?"

I nod once.

"Alessandro too?"

"Not yet, but I will. Ready?"

She's still sitting there and has her arm over whatever is on her desk. I see a corner of something familiar, but before I can think about it, she clears he throat. I return my gaze to hers.

"I just need a minute. I need to pack up a few things. You can have a drink if you want. I'll meet you at the bar?"

She's behaving strangely, and I notice the two tumblers, one empty and one with what I assume is whiskey, on the table in the sitting area. Her lipstick is along the edge of the still full glass. She follows my gaze.

"Father of the bride-to-be needed a drink when he saw the bill." She attempts a chuckle, but it's a poor try.

I study her. "Everything okay?"

"Everything like what?"

"You're acting strange."

She glances down, busies herself with something on her desk. "Just a long night."

"We'll have a drink when we get home. What do you need?" I step toward her.

"Nothing. I'm ready." She quickly slides the large book into her tote and stands.

"What's that?"

"Oh, just some work."

I watch her face. I know she's lying, but I can't figure out why or what she's hiding. There's nothing to hide at this point, is there?

"Okay. Let's go." I gesture to the door, she just barely meets my eyes as she goes through it and out into the lobby. She and the man I stationed in the lobby exchange a strange look. When I go to him, he can't quite meet my eyes. "Everything all right here? Any trouble?"

"No, sir."

"You're new with me, aren't you?"

"Yes, sir."

"Dave Russo, right?"

"Yes, sir."

I watch him a moment longer and see sweat beading on

his forehead. I pat his back a little harder than I need to. "Good to have you, Dave."

When I turn to Emilia, she's watching us. I can't help but wonder if they're sharing some secret. But that makes no sense.

With a hand at her lower back, I lead her out to the waiting car, noting how she's clutching the tote.

"Do you mind if I go to my apartment tonight?"

"I don't think that's a great idea."

"You can't keep me locked up in your house."

"I promised you my protection. I don't break my promises." I open the door, and she slides in. I take the tote from her. She tries to grab it back, and as soon as she does, I pull it just out of reach.

"Heavy."

"I...I wanted to take some of my personal things home."

I hand it to Vincent, my eyes narrow as I study her, watch how she flushes a little when she lies. "Put this in the trunk." He nods and puts it away. A few minutes later, we're on our way back to my house. "Why are you anxious?"

"I'm not."

"What's in the bag?"

She looks me straight in the eye. "Nothing. Just work." She pauses, seems to change her mind. "And I guess I am a little anxious with Alessandro out there, knowing where I am and all."

"You don't have to worry about him. I won't let anything happen to you."

We drive in silence the rest of the way home. Once there, I watch her as I take her bag out of the trunk, carry it in for her.

"Do you want a drink before heading up to bed?" I ask.

She shakes her head. "I have an early day tomorrow."

"All right. Good night, then."

She eyes the tote. "Can I have my bag?"

I shake my head. "You'd better get some sleep. You have an early day tomorrow," I remind her.

She swallows. She knows I know she's lying. "Are you coming upstairs?"

"I have a few calls to make. I'll be up soon."

Conversation is stilted, but she nods and turns to go. "Emilia," I call out once she's on the first-floor landing.

She stops and turns.

"Good night."

"Good night."

I meet Vincent in the kitchen.

"Russo acted strange, don't you think?"

"Yeah. I'll make a point to drop by his place tomorrow. Find out what's going on."

"Good idea."

"What do you want to do with the women?"

I open the fridge and grab a beer for myself and one for him. I drink a third of it before answering. "I'm hoping this will be resolved before the seventy-two hours are up. Right now, I want to see what's in that bag."

I carry the tote into my study and unzip it. Inside I find some folders and among them, a book, the corner of which looked familiar. I lift it out and set it on my desk. I don't want to touch it, but I force myself to, force myself to open the carved wood cover. My mother had had this book specially made when I was born. It was a photo album. Mine. And, as I numbly turn the pages, I see the outline where each of the photos once stood. Each one she painstakingly placed. I wonder if he destroyed them.

"Vincent," I call out, my voice hoarse.

Vincent is at the door in a moment.

"Find out what my father used to bribe Russo." I look up and meet his eyes. "Then kill him."

He glances at the desk, but I doubt he can make out what I'm looking at. He nods his acquiescence and walks away.

I return my attention to the book, make myself read the headlines. I haven't seen most of them, but they all tell the same story. A years-old love triangle. Father and son as rivals over the affections of the beautiful, innocent Angelica. A son who could not let go of the past, long after the tragedy.

Angelica. What I feel at the mention of her name is sorry. Sorry for her.

Although the name didn't always fit the woman. Angel. No, she wasn't that. Not when she started our affair—my education, as she called it—not when she ended it in his bed.

But my father soon showed her his true face. By then, it was too late for her. She was pregnant. Just another woman in a string of affairs my father had had. But this one, I think she did love him. I wonder if he realized it. If he cared.

I didn't know about the pregnancy until years later. Until I found the letter she wrote me before she killed herself. She had reached out to me for help, help against my father, help to keep her baby. But I never responded because I never received the letter. My father intercepted it. He read it and, even hearing the desperation in it, he'd kept it from me. She paid a heavy price for his deception.

That was the letter Emilia found in the library the other day.

When Angelica told my father about the pregnancy, he'd rejected her. Told her she needed to get rid of the baby. Made her go along with it. And the guilt killed her. She'd jumped from the window in the attic of our home in Calabria a few days after the abortion. Four stories. A cliff. Instant death.

After her death, I was sad. Not angry. The anger didn't come until I discovered the letter among my father's things. Then I was angry. Enraged. But it wasn't how the papers printed it—not what Emilia would have read in this book. That's fiction. The story my father told. The real tragedy is in that letter. If it was in English, she'd have read it and understood and this book wouldn't carry the weight it must for her.

I took everything from my father when I learned the truth. Took it all, and put him in a wheelchair to watch life pass him by.

I'm calm when I close the book. Calm still as I climb the stairs to my bedroom.

Emilia is innocent, I know that. But she lied to me. And she still doesn't trust me.

The lights are out in the bedroom, but I know she's awake. I take off my clothes, watching her in the strip of moonlight coming in between the curtains.

"I changed my mind," she says.

"About what?"

"Those men. You're right. It won't do any good for me to see them. I don't want to see them."

"I'll take care of them."

She sits up, meets my eyes. The sheet falls to her lap. She's naked, her hair covering one of her breasts, leaving the other exposed. She's so beautiful. And still, after everything, so out of reach.

"You mean you'll kill them," she says matter-of-factly.

I go to her. Stand over her. "Yes." My gaze settles on her

breast, then lower to the crease of her thigh. Her sex is covered by the sheet.

She looks up at me, then down over me, over my chest, abs, her eyes coming to rest on my cock.

"Get on your hands and knees."

I hear her breath quicken, and she licks her lips. But then she turns her gaze up to mine and asks me a question that shouldn't surprise me.

"Are you going to hurt me, Giovanni?"

I study her, this strange, beautiful, damaged girl. She must know I've gone through her bag.

"I said hands and knees, Emilia. Facing me."

She climbs up on all fours, and I take a handful of her hair in my hands, make her look at me while I look at her like this.

I take my time before returning my eyes to hers. "Are you a liar, Emilia?"

She swallows, tries to shake her head no, but I don't give her any room to because that's the wrong answer. I bring her face to my cock, push into her mouth, pump in and out twice, three times, then pull out.

"Are you a liar?"

"No."

"Then why do you lie to me?" I push in again, all the way this time, making her choke, keeping her down when she tries to push back, pumping, touching the back of her throat.

When I pull out, she has tears on her face and is gasping for breath.

"I'm going to ask you this exactly once. Is there something you should tell me?"

She shakes her head no.

"Fine. Turn around. Face in the bed, ass high."

She turns, gets into the position I require of her. When I press down on her lower back, she arches it, and I can see all of her now. My hands move to cup her ass, spread her wider. She's shaved everything.

"I like you like this. Did he like it too? My father? Did you show him too?"

"What? No!"

I hold her in place when she tries to move, slap her ass.

"Did you get on all fours for him?"

She pulls away. I let her this time. She turns to me.

"No. Why would you say that? No. God. No."

I point to the space before me. "Get back up. Now."

"No. What is wrong with you?"

"I said up, damnit."

She tries to scramble backward, but I grab her ankle and tug her to me so that she's flat on the bed.

"Leave me alone!"

"You're mine. Not his. You're going to remember that after tonight. Get. Up." I flip her over, slap her ass again, and drag her hips to me.

"Stop it! You're hurting me."

"I thought you liked that."

She kicks her leg back, just missing my balls. I grab her and haul her up so she's kneeling up on the bed. "That was a mistake."

"Did you hurt her?" she blurts out.

I stop.

"Is it true? Did you?" I let her go.

It's like a slap in the face. I feel her words like a physical assault, and it takes me some time to process. I shake my head. These words, they impact me more than I care to admit. More than I thought I could be impacted.

"You ask me if it's fucking true?"

She's watching me, crying a little. I get on the bed, grip her hair, and tug her head backward.

"How can you ask me that?" I'm calm. My heartbeat is level in the face of this betrayal.

She looks up at me, and I see so much sadness in her eyes, confusion and trust that's been broken again and again and again. And I can't blame her.

"I never hurt her. Not like he said. Not like they printed. I wouldn't, not her, not anyone. I thought you'd know that about me." I shouldn't care what she thinks. Why do I? I should just put her back on her hands and knees and fuck her. That's all she should be to me.

But instead, I release her and get off the bed. I don't feel like a fuck anymore. I find my pants and pull them on and walk to the bedroom door.

"I shouldn't want you," she says, stopping me when I reach it.

"Don't worry. I'll make it easy for you." I put my hand on the door handle.

"You're not good."

"I don't think you're looking for good." I step back into the room. "I think you're self-destructing. I think you've been hanging on by the thinnest thread for so long, you can't even see straight anymore. You can't see good or bad, and you're so fucking scared to let go of that illusion of control you think you have that it leaves you empty and alone. Let me tell you something. You have none. You have *zero* control. You need to stop running and face the past. Face yourself and move the fuck on."

"Move on? You think I haven't tried? You think I don't make myself look in the mirror every single day? Make myself count every single line on my back every single fucking day? I was raped!" She chokes on that word. "I was raped by *five men*. Five men my brother arranged to rape me while he watched. While he took fucking photos. I'm not sure there's anything sicker than that, and you think I should *move the fuck on*?"

Her face crumples as she says it, and I wonder if that last seam isn't coming apart now. That final thread finally ripping.

"Do you have any idea how hard—how fucking impossible—it is for me to get up out of bed every morning? Do you think you know what it's like to be betrayed like I was?" She's talking through sobs. "And yet you want me to trust you, but it's not like you tell me anything, is it? Not like you tell me anything when I ask. You just tell me I have to trust you. How can I?"

"I didn't rape Angelica. I didn't impregnate her then abandon her. My father did that. And when she reached out to me for help, I wasn't there because he made sure I never heard her cry." I stalk to her, take her by the arms, and shake her hard. "You asked me if I wanted to save you because I couldn't save her and I don't know. Maybe I do. I don't fucking know. But you fucking sit here and tell me you still don't trust me. Let me ask you this. How many times do I have to save you for you to learn? For you to see that you *can* trust me? How many times do I have to come after you for you to see that I'm not going to let you go? That I won't let you drown? How. Many. Times."

"Why?" she asks, her voice small, her face that of the frightened, lost, little girl again. "Why do you keep doing it?"

"Because..." Fuck. I can't finish.

"Why do you keep bothering with me? I'm broken. There's nothing left to break. You said it yourself. Why fucking bother? I'm damaged goods. How can you want that?"

It's quiet for a second. Just the sound of a sniffle from her.

"Because as fucked-up as it is, maybe I want to fix you." I let her go, feel her slip from my grasp. "Unbreak you."

She lets out a choked sob. "You can't unbreak something. It doesn't work that way." Her voice cracks. She wipes the back of her hand across her face. "But you're wrong about one thing, you know that?" She collapses onto the bed like her knees can't support her anymore.

I look down at her. She's quieter. Tears slide down her cheeks and turn her eyes and the tip of her nose red and she's licking them from her lips.

"You're wrong," she says again. "There is more to break. And I'm scared you're going to be the one to do it. To shatter what's left of me."

I watch her, her pretty green eyes so sad now.

No, not just now. Always. Always sad.

She bows her head, and I see tears fall and land on the bed. Emilia, small and alone in my bed.

21

EMILIA

I must look so pathetic to him. So weak. I half expect him to walk away, walk out the door. Leave me here, a sad, miserable mess.

But then he does something that surprises me. He crouches down and wraps one arm around me. I feel his warmth, his strength. Giovanni pulls me into him, and I let him. I let myself fall into him. My head is in the crook of his neck and my tears are wet on his skin and I feel myself tremble. Hear myself sob. And it's different than before. Different than any other time. This time, I'm giving my pain. Letting someone else carry it for a little while.

He holds me like this for a long time, and when I quiet, he says my name, turns my face up to his. He kisses me, and I wonder if he tastes the salt of my tears on my lips when he does. I kiss him back. He lifts me in his arms and lays me on the bed, and I cling to him. I don't want to be apart from him. I can't get close enough to him

My hands slip from his neck because I want more. I need more. I undo his pants and push them down and he's between my legs and then he's filling me up. He's inside me, and it's all that matters. This. Right now. Us. Him and me. Him inside me.

"I don't want to hurt you. Break you. I fucking love you," he says. It's a whisper, and the words sound so strange on his tongue.

I put my hands on his face. I want to see him, see his eyes, and I know in that instant, I can't ever be without him. I don't close my eyes when I kiss him, and he moves inside me, fucking me, his breath coming shorter as I cling to him, wrap my legs around him, want him deeper still. I know he feels me come. He was waiting for that because I feel him throb inside me then. I look at him, and his face is just inches from mine. We come together, and I think neither of us wants it to end.

He holds me afterward. I think about what he said. About fixing me. Unbreaking me.

It's like he reads my mind. "I want to amend what I said," he pauses. "I don't want to fix you. I'll take you exactly as you are. All the broken pieces of you."

I smile a little. "I didn't believe all that about you. I don't even know why I asked you. I should have told you your father came to see me."

He just gives a short nod, but his eyes harden at the mention of the old man.

"You aren't going to follow through with your threat?" I suddenly remember it.

"That business is between me and my father."

"Giovanni, don't. It's not worth it. He's not worth it."

He doesn't answer. I relax again, realizing I had tensed up when the conversation had taken that turn. I change the subject.

"Can I ask you something?"

"I don't want to talk about my father."

"It's not about that."

He raises an eyebrow.

"When we were at that safe house, where my father was. Did I...say it out loud?"

A smile spreads across his face. "You mean did you tell me you loved me?"

I open my mouth to speak, to tell him to wipe that grin off his face, but just then, there's an urgent knock on the door and Vincent calls out. Giovanni's smile vanishes in an instant.

Giovanni moves fast, getting up, pulling on a pair of jeans, and opening the door in mere seconds. He steps into the hallway but doesn't close the door all the way.

"What is it?"

"We got him on camera. He was just at her apartment."

"What? Where are the men I put there?"

I sit up, holding the blanket to myself.

Vincent shakes his head, shrugs.

"Fuck! Get more men out there. I'll be right down."

Vincent nods and leaves. Giovanni is pulling on a T-shirt he snagged off the back of a chair and disappears into his closet.

"Is it Alessandro?"

He returns, loading a cartridge into a pistol. He looks at me. Nods.

I get out of the bed, go to him. "Don't kill him, okay?" I don't know why I ask that.

He just looks at me, doesn't answer my question. And I know he *will* kill him. "I have to go."

"Be careful. He's got nothing to lose."

"I know." He pulls me close, studies my face for a long moment like he's memorizing it, like it may be the last time he sees me, and worry settles into my belly. But then he lets me go. "Stay here, Emilia."

I nod. He's gone an instant later.

"No one touches him but me, understood?" he calls out in the hallway.

He's gone. I'm still trying to register what's happened. I sit back down on the bed and pull the covers up to my lap. I'm thinking.

Alessandro is here. He was in my apartment. I knew Giovanni was watching it. I think it's strange my brother didn't realize that he would be. Alessandro is more devious than that. More cunning. He should have known.

I feel anxious. Alessandro so close. *In* my apartment. What if I'd been there? I'm glad now that Giovanni wouldn't let me go home earlier. I do wish he'd taken me with him now, though. I could help, and, if it came to it, protect Giovanni from Alessandro. Not that I think he needs protecting. Giovanni will crush my brother.

But something isn't sitting right with me.

The bed is still warm from our lovemaking. What happened just now, I need time to process it. I think about that night at the safehouse, when Giovanni was there, when he came for me. He confronted me about it then. Fearlessly. I thought that was it. That my secret was out, that it was over. But tonight, me saying the word. Saying out loud that terrible word—I think that may have been the first real step I've taken in moving forward, in taking control of this rather than letting it control me. Letting it define me. Own me.

"I don't want to fix you. I'll take you exactly as you are. All the broken pieces of you."

I push the covers back and get out of bed. I can't lose myself in his words. This isn't a fairy tale. People like us, we don't get happily-ever-after.

I go into the bathroom, switch on the shower. Something keeps nagging at me about Alessandro having gone to my apartment. I assume he got word about me from one of the men from the other night at the club. I assume they told him Giovanni had me. Or did they say that I was on Giovanni's arm? It certainly would have appeared so. It wouldn't have looked like I was there against my will, not like them. If they got word to Alessandro, he would come for me. I wonder if his hate for me is greater than his sense of self-preservation?

When the water begins to steam, I step under the flow. I use Giovanni's shampoo, his soap, and I can smell him around me. On me.

After the shower, I get dressed and go downstairs. I'm looking for my bag. My phone is inside, and I want to call Nan. I know it's late, but I want her to know Alessandro is here, that Giovanni will pick him up tonight, and that she and dad are safe. That soon we won't need to hide anymore.

After checking in the kitchen, I go to his study, where I find the door ajar. I push it open all the way and spot the book his father had given me on his desk. Blood betrayal. It's the worst kind.

I shift my gaze away from it. I was right in my initial reaction to the old man. There is something vile about him.

My tote is sitting beside the desk on the floor. I pick it up, dig through it to find my phone, which is switched off. It must have run out of batteries. I look around for a charger. It's an iPhone, although it's an older one, so I think Giovanni must have a charger that fits. The unlocked drawers don't contain one, though. I don't try the one that was locked the other day. I know what's inside that one.

I go into the kitchen and start to look through the drawers there. Everyone has a catch-all drawer. I try several before I find his and inside it, a charger that will work. I plug it in and wait until I can turn it on. And I see a blinking light go on right away, telling me I have a voice message.

My heartbeat picks up because no one knows this number. Only Nan. Did I miss her call again? Did something happen to dad?

I push the message button, and it takes three tries for me to remember my password. There's silence for a long time, so long that I almost delete the message, thinking it was a mistake. But something tells me not to. Maybe it's that background noise because there's something familiar about it. Something that makes every hair on my body stand on end.

"I moved daddy," the low, mocking voice finally says. There's a slow chuckle. "You got that one by me, I'll admit." Silence. No, not silence. That noise again. It's louder this time. And I go rigid, my hand trembling so badly I almost drop the phone. Because that sound, it's me. It's familiar because it's me.

It cuts out, then starts again and I know he's moved the recording forward. Because I was still screaming in the initial part. Still fighting. Now I'm not. Now I'm whimpering. He moves it again, and the sound of leather breaking flesh makes me jump. The scream that follows makes my blood run cold.

He recorded it too. I didn't know. Photos weren't enough for him. I wonder if he's replayed this over the years. Relived my suffering. My breaking.

"But Nan," his voice says. "Poor Nan. She'd gotten old, huh? I'm sorry to say she didn't make it, Sis."

"What?"

No one answers. It's just a recording.

"Now, dad's not looking so good, is he?" I hear the sound of machine's beeping. My father's machines. "Crazy. I can stick a pin right into his eye, and he doesn't even flinch."

"Stop!"

"You have one hour to get your ass here. One hour, and you'd better be alone, or I'll be putting more than pins in his eyes." There's rage in his tone. It combats the violence of his words. But when he speaks again, it's in that laid-back, mocking tone. "You can figure out where, I suppose?" He turns up the recording. Leather on flesh. Screams. The laughter of men.

Then, abruptly, a woman comes on. It takes me a minute to realize what it is. "If you'd like to delete the message, press..."

I hang up and immediately dial Nan's number. There's no answer. Did I expect there to be one? But how did Alessandro get past Giovanni's men?

Same way he got past them at my apartment, I guess.

I open the door that leads to the garage. It's unlocked, but I guess Giovanni isn't expecting I'll leave, not after tonight.

God. Tonight. How can something so perfect turn into the worst night of my life?

No, not the worst. I lived those nights. This isn't the worst.

But maybe by the time it's over, it will be.

I don't know if I'm expecting to find a car in the garage, but I don't. Giovanni took it, obviously. I go back into the kitchen and through the hallway to the front door. It's locked, and I need a key to open it. Shit! I walk to the French doors that lead out to the garden, but I can see already that he's secured the door I shot out.

"Think. Damn it, think!" I try Nan's number again. Again there's no answer. I go back into the kitchen, lose ten minutes looking through every drawer for a key, finding none. I try the garage and realize I can manually open the door.

It takes me a few minutes to figure out how to do it, but then the door starts to go up. Once it's halfway, I run underneath it and hail a taxi. Remarkably, one stops right away. I get in and give him the address of the house, the one I never wanted to go back to. Never wanted to see. But I have no choice.

The driver stops, turns back to me, then glances at the house I just stepped out of. "You sure you want to go to that neighborhood, lady? I don't think—"

"Please go as fast as you can!"

"All right. Suit yourself. Try to help someone out..."

I block him out and try to call Nan again. She can't be dead. He can't have killed her. "Oh, God, Nan, answer. Please answer."

But she doesn't and I hang up and think about the fact that I should have grabbed a kitchen knife, looked for a gun, fuck, something. I stupidly came with nothing. No weapon. I should call Giovanni. Tell him where I'm going. Where to find Alessandro, because he's on the wrong path. Alessandro isn't at my apartment. Alessandro only sent him there to separate us because he knows I'll come, and he knows Giovanni would never let me come alone. My brother has nothing to lose now. His days are numbered; they have been since he decided to double cross Giovanni. And I know he's going to try to take Nan, my father, and me with him.

The night seems darker as we near the neighborhood, and I know why the taxi driver was warning me. I do know this neighborhood well.

"Here. Stop here."

He stops down the street from the house. My eyes are

locked on it. It's dark, like no one is home. Like no one has been home for years. Is this where Alessandro was holed up?

I open the car door as soon as the taxi stops, and the cabbie catches my wrist. "Whoa, hold on there, lady." He points to the fare machine.

"Shit. I forgot my wallet."

He gives me an incredulous look. I have an idea. "Go back to the house where you picked me up. Keep the meter running. They'll pay you. Ask for Giovanni. He'll be looking for me. Give him this address."

"Are you sending me on some wild-goose chase?"

"No, I swear. I have to go. Please, just do this. I promise you'll be paid for all your trouble. Please."

"What's your name?"

"Emilia. Emilia Estrella."

He studies me, narrows his eyes. "You sure you should be here?"

I nod. I have to be.

He releases me. "All right, Emilia. But if this Giovanni don't pay up, I'm coming for you," he says, any concern or kindness for me gone from his tone.

I step out into the night and close the door while he mutters something under his breath. I watch the taxi disappear down the road, and I'm truly alone. I make my way down the broken sidewalk to that broken house where four years ago, a broken girl emerged from a cracked basement window, her body and spirit as fractured as the sidewalk of this forgotten neighborhood.

22

EMILIA

My steps slow as I near the property. I don't want to go inside. I don't want to be here. But I have no choice. I wonder if the taxi driver will get word to Giovanni in time.

In time.

Before my brother finishes the job he started four years ago. Before he kills me.

I finally stand before the run-down house. I stop and stare at the front door, eye each of the dark windows. The lawn is overrun with weeds, and they're creeping up through the cracks of the walkway too. I take the first step, then another. My heart is racing, and I realize I'm saying a prayer.

When I reach the door, I simply stand there and wait. He knows I'm here.

A moment later, the lock turns and the door opens. The remembered smell of the house overwhelms me. Makes me take a step back.

A calloused hand appears from the blackness inside and closes around my wrist. Alessandro steps into what dim light the streetlamp offers and, for the first time in four years, I see him. I see my twin brother. And I don't recognize him.

He's wearing a deep red T-shirt. The name of the band featured on it is so faded I can't make it out. His hair is shaggy, and his beard is overgrown. I can see bits of food in it. He gives me a one-sided grin and cocks his head, making a point of looking me over from head to toe and back.

"Well, well, sister. Fucking the enemy seems to agree with you."

With that, he tugs me inside. I let out a small scream as the door slams shut behind me. Despite the weight he's lost, he's still so strong. He always was.

"Where's daddy?"

"Aww, how cute. You still call him daddy," he mocks, not releasing me as he pulls me toward the door that leads downstairs. Down to that basement. He opens it.

I dig my heels in. I'm looking around, straining my ears to hear any sound, but there's nothing.

"Where is he?" He's not here. I don't see his bed. I don't hear machines.

And I realize something.

He isn't here.

He was never here.

Alessandro watches me with a grin on his face as I put the pieces together and understand.

"If I tell you he's downstairs, will you head down on your own? Cause that's where you and me are going."

"Get off me. Let me go!"

He chuckles and drags me forward. "Or I can just hurl you down if you want."

I have no doubt he would.

He flips the switch, and the lights blink on downstairs.

He pulls me onto the stairs, then turns to lock the door and pockets the key. He heads down with me in tow, and I remember the familiar creak of the step that's third from the bottom. Remember how it used to wake me up. Alert me to their return. I slept easily then too. Seemed to constantly sleep.

Only once we're down the stairs does he release me.

"You are so stupid, Sis. I mean, *think*."

I back away, looking around, remembering everything. Everything exactly as it had been. They haven't even cleaned the dried blood on the floor and the whip he used, it's hanging on the wall as if ready and waiting to do its job again.

My eyes are locked on that when he backs me into a corner and pokes his finger into my forehead.

"Really, use your fucking brain. You have one, right? Isn't that why *daddy* spent all that money on tutors for you? Or was it because you're slow? I mean, the old man is on fucking machines. How in hell would I have moved him without *unplugging* him? You always were so damn stupid."

"You don't have him. You never did. What about Nan?"

"Never say never, you know better. She taught us that, didn't she? Yeah, I think it was Nan."

"Where is she?"

He shrugs a shoulder. "Morgue? No, too soon for that. Lying in her blood on the kitchen floor?"

I step toward him. "If you hurt her—"

He pushes me backward. "What? If I hurt her, what?"

"Just tell me she's okay! You have me here, what more do you want?"

"First of all, if I told you she was okay, that would be a lie, and I don't want to lie. You know I don't like it. Second, what more do I want? Are you really asking that?"

"They're coming for you. Giovanni's coming."

"Really?" He stops and pretends he's listening at the window, the one I crept out of four years ago. It's been repaired. Sort of. It's boarded up. I know that won't be my exit tonight. "I don't hear him."

"If you hurt me, he'll kill you."

"He'll kill me either way. Why not take you with me? No reason not to. Misery loves company and all that."

He stops, leans forward, and sniffs me.

"You stink of sex, you know that? No amount of soap can cover that up, Sis. Never could get enough, could you? My sister, the whore."

He puts his hands on me, tears the blouse I'm wearing down the middle.

"Stop! Alessandro. You're my brother."

"Don't worry. I'm not planning on fucking you. That's sick. Not that I remember you being very picky. It's disgusting to watch your sister come with some filthy dick in her filthy cunt, you know that?"

I feel myself cave in a little. Shrink away a little.

"Touchy still? Aww. Poor baby." He tugs on my shirt again, tearing it from me this time and, gripping my arm, he pulls me roughly to the center of the room where the cuffs still hang from the chain.

"Stop, Alessandro, stop."

I fight but he is so much stronger than he should be. I think that's what happens when you know this is it.

He raises one of my arms over my head and clicks the cuff into place around my wrist. I grip the chain and try to hit him with my free hand but only manage to scratch his face, which pisses him off. He stops and steps back.

I stop too, and look at the four streaks of blood on his cheek. His breathing becomes tighter. I can see his anger burning, growing, bubbling over, and before I can think, he slaps me so hard that I see stars. My cheek throbs with pain. I feel him take my left arm, which is now hanging limp at my side, and drag it up until he snaps the other cuff around it.

"You're such a cunt," he mutters. He's moving away, but I hear him.

I blink, force my eyes to open. I'm just hanging now, my weight suspended. He's torn away my shirt so I'm in a bra and jeans. My shoes have slipped off somewhere. I turn to look for them, I don't know why, but then I hear a familiar sound. A terrifying one.

"I'm going to whip you raw front and back," he says. "Then I'm going to peel away your skin before I put you out of your misery."

"You don't have to do this, Alessandro. You don't."

"I know I don't," he says, walking around me, coming behind me so close that I feel his hot breath on the side of my face. He pushes my hair over my shoulder to expose my back, touches it, traces a scar. "But I want to."

And before I can open my mouth to get another word out, the first lash falls across my back.

23

GIOVANNI

"It's a fucking setup. We've been played."

I walk around that fucking apartment for the twentieth time, looking for any clue he might have left, cursing at the men on duty, fucking sleeping on the job to have let him through.

The camera shows Alessandro Estrella, thinner than I remember, bearded, his hair looking like he needed it cut half a year ago, taking his time as he walks around Emilia's home. He drinks her whiskey before pouring the remainder of its contents all over her carpet, her furniture. He eats her food, leaving packages lying around as he does. Opens drawers, moves things, even goes through her bedroom, her underwear drawer. It's sick, actually. This is her brother, and he's making my stomach turn.

I sent a man back to the house as soon as I realized what was going on. And when it rains, it fucking pours. I just got a call telling me her father went into cardiac arrest.

I'm heading out the front door of her building when Vincent's phone rings. He stops and turns to me.

"She's not there. She's not at the house, and there's a taxi driver demanding payment."

"What?" I take the phone. "This is Giovanni. What the hell is happening?"

"The garage door was half up when I got here, so I searched the house, but I barely got through the second floor when a taxi driver shows up, saying he gave the woman who lives here a ride. She didn't have her wallet and sent him back here to find you. Asked for you by name."

"Where did he take her?"

He's talking to the driver as Vincent and I get into the car.

"Let me talk to him myself!" I bark.

A moment later the driver is on the line. "She was real upset. I'll be honest, I didn't want to leave here there alone."

"But you fucking did. Address. I need the fucking address."

"Am I getting paid?"

"You're going to get a bullet in your head if I don't get the fucking address."

He spells it out, and I'm already driving. I know the neighborhood, and she doesn't belong anywhere near it.

"He fucking played us. We should have known."

Vincent is making calls, getting men out to the house. I've got the pedal to the floor, but we're not going to make it in time. She's been there alone too long. He's had her too long.

"Fuck!"

"We've got an army coming for him. We'll get him."

It's not getting him I'm concerned with. It's the damage he'll do in the meantime.

"She can't fucking stay put. Not fucking once."

A mixture of rage and fury drive me on. Somehow we make it to the neighborhood, to that house, without incident. Several cars screech to a stop behind us. I pull my weapon, ready it. Vincent sends men around the back of the house, and he's flanking me.

It's quiet, too quiet. I try the door but it's locked. Of course it's fucking locked. The house looks empty. Abandoned.

But what if this isn't right? What if she isn't here?

Aiming my weapon, I shoot out the lock. If she is here, we've just lost the element of surprise. We charge inside, my men fanning out through the house. The door at the far end catches my eye. It's got a lock on it, a very heavy lock meant for outdoor use. I go to it, and that's when I hear it. Hear the crack of a whip. Hear her scream.

I don't think then. All I hear is that scream. I shoot through the lock and charge down the stairs and I see her. I see her in the center of the room, strung up like she must have been years before. There's a bruise on her cheekbone and a cut on her lip. Her face is wet with tears. The whip is on the floor, but I can't see the damage he's done because he's got her back to his front, a knife at her throat, and every time he moves, I see her fist her hands and hear her pain.

"You're a dead man, Estrella." There are three pistols pointed at him, but my men know not to fire until I give the word. And this prick is using her as a shield. "Let her go, and I'll make it quick."

"I'd rather you watch her bleed out. That'll be worth whatever you do to me. Or I walk out of here, and you get her in roughly the same condition she was in when she got here."

No way he's walking out of here tonight.

I meet her desperate eyes, take a step toward the pair.

"Stay back. I mean it. I'll kill her."

"I don't think you will," I say, taking another step. He touches the tip of his blade to her throat, and a droplet of blood slides down it. She squeezes her eyes shut, squeezes out more tears. I'm going to extract double what she cried. I'm going to make it so slow, he'll be begging me to kill him before I'm through.

"Oh, I mean it," he says as I take another step. He tries to take one back, but he can't because of her bonds.

"Don't you find it a little pathetic you come after your sister, again, all because daddy loved her more than you?" I step closer yet, see Vincent getting into position from the corner of my eye. "I mean, a true betrayal, that I understand. But what did she do to you really?"

He just keeps his eyes locked on mine but he's jittery, anxious. Even if he got a gun and made a dash for the stairs, even if he managed to hit one of us, the others would take him out. He has to know this.

"Move away from her. I'm not going to say it again."

"I'll drive the blade into her throat if you come closer."

I give a shake of my head, and there' a crash at the far end of the basement. Vincent just turned a table over, and that's the instant of distraction I need to lunge at him. I grab his wrist and tug it away from her throat, then shove him back. He's stronger than I expect, given his size, but he's no match for me. For my rage.

I don't release his wrist when his back hits the wall. Instead, I twist it, turning the blade toward his throat, slicing it just a little, shallow enough not to kill him, but I do draw blood. He lets out a whimper. Like the coward he is.

Relieving him of the blade, I lean in close. Hold my nose against the stench of him. "Don't be a fucking pussy." Taking his arm, I shove him toward Vincent, who holds him.

I turn to look at Emilia. She's shaking. I go to her and reach up for the bonds. I glance at her back before I release her. It's bloody, but it's not twenty-one. He managed three lashes. Three angry lashes.

She falls into me when I release her, and I hold her, careful for her back. I want to lift her up in my arms, but it'll hurt her if I do.

"String him up," I say, moving her toward the stairs. "You're going to be okay," I tell her. It's not a question. She will be okay. She has to be. "You're safe now."

"Nan and my dad?"

Fuck.

She draws back when I don't answer. "Did he get to them?" she asks, her face crumpling again. "He said he got to them."

I shake my head. "No, he didn't. It's not that."

"What then?"

"Your father went into cardiac arrest a little while ago."

She shakes her head no, more tears coming. I push the hair from her face. It's stuck to it with blood and sweat. I inadvertently touch the bruise, making her flinch. "Shh. I'll get you cleaned up, and we'll go to them. Can you walk?"

She nods.

"Good." I turn to Alessandro, who is now bound in the same restraints from which I freed Emilia. "I'll be back for him," I say to Vincent but keep my eyes on Alessandro. I won't be delivering him to my cousin in the condition he wants—alive. Not a fucking chance. "You boys can warm him up."

Emilia has her eyes locked on him too.

"Let's go," I say.

"Wait."

She pushes my arm away, goes up to her brother, walks

right up to him, and I'm not sure what to expect. I hope she won't beg for his life because I'm not granting that. But she doesn't. Instead, she spits in his face.

"You're a pathetic, sick coward, and you deserve everything they're going to do to you."

EPILOGUE 1

EMILIA

Seven Weeks Later

Alessandro had lied about Nan and my father. He hadn't gotten to them. Giovanni has an army surrounding them. Even if he had known where they were, he wouldn't have gotten through.

Nan is sitting beside me now as I look at dad. It's almost like he knew what was happening, what Alessandro was doing to me, because I think his heart stopped at the same time I was in that basement. It's almost like he was there with me. Already an angel watching over me.

I wipe my face and squeeze his hand, look at him. Look at the additional machines. He could breathe on his own before. Not anymore.

Nan is crying too. This whole thing, it's aged her. And my dad, I wouldn't recognize him for my father if I didn't know it was him. He's a shadow of the man he was in life.

Life.

He's not alive anymore. Not really. He's not here inside this body anymore. I know that.

I don't need to look up to know Giovanni is watching me from across the room. I stand up, lean over my dad, and give him one more kiss on his forehead. Nan does the same. She and I hold hands.

"You're doing the right thing, Emilia," she reassures me.

"I know. It's still hard."

I take another minute and look up at the doctor, give him a nod. One by one, he switches off the machines. One by one, the noises stop. And as they do, I watch my father's face. I want to say I see peace on it, even if it's only my imagination. His chest stops moving as soon as that machine is turned off and a few minutes later, the doctor calls out the time of death.

It should be easier if you know. It shouldn't hurt so much if you know. I feel like I've done this twice now. Lost him twice.

Nan rubs my arm, and I steel myself, force myself to stop with the crying. I have to stop sometime. It's been four long years of it, and I'm so tired of crying all the time. I lean down and give him one final kiss and tell him that I love him. When Giovanni comes to take my hand and lead me away, I go. I don't wait for them to put the sheet over his face. I don't want to see that.

It's been seven weeks since that terrible night. My back is healed, and now, twenty-four lines mark it. My age. It doesn't mean anything, though.

I don't know what Giovanni did to my brother. I don't ask, and he doesn't tell. I don't know what he did to those other men either, but I know they're all dead now. The women he released. He kept his promise and didn't lay a finger on them.

I look over at him, squeeze his hand. I was wrong when I told him he wasn't good. He is. In his own way.

"You did the right thing," he says to me once we're in the car.

"You were right. I just didn't want to see it."

"I have some meetings in Italy next week. I want you to come with me," he says as we head into the city. "After the funeral. Let's just get out of here. Take a break."

I look over at him. "Like a vacation?" It's strange. We're talking like we're a normal couple or something.

"Yeah, sort of. I need to meet with some of the local men who worked for my father."

"Worked?"

"They work for me now. There were some mixed loyalties. I want to be sure everyone is on the same page."

I know it's not as civilized as that.

"Can I ask you what happened with your father?" I'm cautious when I bring it up. All I know is Giovanni paid him a visit a few weeks ago. When he came back, he seemed different. Not as angry or something.

He studies me. "Let's leave that between him and me. You don't need to know that part of my life."

"It's part of my life if I'm with you."

He smiles, like he likes what I said. "You're clean, Emilia. I plan on keeping you that way. You'll come with me to Calabria."

"I have a job, you know."

"You can take time off. I want you there."

I study him, and he studies me back. As much as I pretend to be annoyed by it, I like his dominance. It makes me feel safe.

"I've never been to Italy."

EPILOGUE 2
GIOVANNI

The trip to Calabria is a necessary one. It's not a vacation, not for me. And this place, there are memories here. Ghosts of the past.

When I met with my father after things settled down for Emilia, I learned some things. Amazing what you can get out of a man who is desperate to keep all his limbs—and for the record, he didn't. Because he needed to learn once and for all. Because being made to sit in a fucking wheelchair didn't teach him.

I need to be here to settle some rumblings, cement loyalties. Not everyone was happy about how I took over the Santa Maria family. My father can spin an incredible tale, and his lies turned many against me.

My father had been head of the Santa Maria family until shortly after Franco Benedetti's death. In fact, it was soon after he pledged our allegiance to Dominic Benedetti that I learned the truth about Angelica. That letter she wrote me before she jumped, he'd taken it. Hidden it. But he should have destroyed it.

She'd reached out for help, and when I hadn't come,

she'd assumed I'd abandoned her too. That's why she'd killed herself. And it makes it doubly my father's fault.

When I learned the truth years after her death, it took me right back to that time.

But I avenged her by putting him in that wheelchair. By taking his family from him. By taking everything from him and leaving him powerless.

Now I'll be sure to put an end to anyone who challenges my authority, both in the States and in Italy. I'm not a good man. I know who I am, and I don't pretend to be anyone else. But I'm not a liar. I don't steal souls, and I don't hurt innocents.

"This is so beautiful," Emilia says. She's sitting beside me as we ride up the rocky, narrow road to my house. The house is situated on a steep cliff a little outside of Tropea with spectacular views of the sea.

"It's one of the most beautiful places in the world." I take the turns easily, driving a little faster than I probably should, but liking it. I spend most of my time in the States, but my heart is here.

The house comes into view a few minutes later, an ancient stone structure. It's huge and has been in my family for generations. It's always passed on to the first-born male heir. Sexist, I know, but these are the rules and there is enough money to go around.

"Wow."

I glance over at Emilia. She's got her face plastered to the window, taking in everything she can. The sun is high. She's wearing a pretty summer dress and flip-flops and to anyone looking on, we're a normal couple here on vacation.

We pass through the old iron gates, and a few minutes later, I stop the car in front of the house. Remy, the man who runs the household, steps out the front door before we're even out of the car. I come around to open Emilia's door, watch his face as he does a double take. Remy has been working for my family since before I was born, and he knew Angelica. He quickly schools his features, though, and greets us. I introduce Emilia, and we head inside.

The house has been updated over the years. Although it's been kept in the traditional style, it contains all of the comforts of modern life. From the entrance, the foyer opens up into a huge circular hall with stone stairs leading to the second level on either side and, straight through, two large doors that lead to the terrace stand open, where deep purple bougainvillea hang like a canopy overhead, filtering the sun.

"Wow."

"I'll show you," I say, unable to hide my own smile. She's impressed. Anyone who is invited into the house is.

I lead her out onto the terrace, which spans the length of the house. She walks to the farthest point and peeks over the stone railing. The sea is below, the color a deep turquoise.

"You're going to have to learn how to swim." I turn and take out my phone to check messages.

I reply to the message, confirming the time of the meeting, and tuck the phone away.

"Work already?"

I wrap an arm around her. "Not yet. Not until tomorrow. Just have to make a call. Go change into a swimsuit. I'll meet you by the pool. Remy will show you our room."

Remy, ever attentive, is already there.

Her face loses its smile for a moment, but she relinquishes and disappears up the stairs. I head to my study to make the calls, arrangements for tomorrow's meetings. There will be two, one for those loyal to me, and one for those still loyal to my father. It's the latter that worries me. I want those men rounded up and present. I'm not wasting my time here, and they'll be asked exactly once if they're in or out. I assume it will take one example of "out" to cement allegiance. Some people just need a nudge to make the right decision.

Once that's done, and before I go out to meet Emilia, there's one other thing I want to do. Taking a handful of the flowers from the vase in the foyer, I head upstairs, all the way upstairs to the attic. The last time I did this was after what happened with my father. Before the arrest. I still had splatters of my father's blood on my shirt then, the betrayal fresh. I still felt something when I walked up these narrower stairs to the dark room used for storage.

The door at the top of the stairs is locked, but the key is above the door frame. There's not much need for anyone to come up here, and I know the maids think her ghost still haunts it. But I don't think that's true anymore. It did, but it doesn't anymore.

I walk inside. The heat here is stifling. I clear a cobweb out of my path and make my way to a tall, narrow door leading to a small balcony. It creaks open, the hinges rusting. I'll need to make sure that's repaired.

I step out onto the balcony and look down over the cliffs and into the sea. Without a word, I toss the handful of flowers out and watch them as they fall through the sky.

"What are you doing?"

I turn to find Emilia watching me. She's wearing a bikini with a sarong wrapped around her hips and flip–flops. She's holding a wide-brimmed hat and a book in one hand.

"You're sneaky."

"Not sneaky. Just quiet" She studies me, peers over the balcony. "Is this where she..."

"Yes."

Epilogue 2

Again, she watches me, and I watch her.

"Is it weird I'm here?" she asks as if she read my mind.

I thought it might be strange having her here. Here in the same house where she looks so much like the ghost who only recently left the premises. But it's not.

I look her over, the turquoise suit matching the sea, accentuating her olive skin. My hand looks enormous when I set it against her stomach, push her gently backward into the wall. I kiss her.

"You're where you belong. With me."

"But—"

"The past is dead, Emilia. You're my future. And I don't plan on wasting one minute of it."

The faintest smile softens her features and when I take her into my arms, she melts into me, her body molding to mine.

"I love you," I tell her.

"I love you, Giovanni."

The end

SAMPLE FROM TAKEN
DARK LEGACY

Helena

I'm the oldest of the Willow quadruplets. Four girls. Always girls. Every single quadruplet birth, generation after generation, it's always girls.

This generation's crop yielded the usual, but instead of four perfect, beautiful dolls, there were three.

And me.

And today, our twenty-first birthday, is the day of harvesting.

That's the Scafoni family's choice of words, not ours. At least not mine. My parents seem much more comfortable with it than my sisters and I do, though.

Harvesting is always on the twenty-first birthday of the quads. I don't know if it's written in stone somewhere or what, but it's what I know and what has been on the back of my mind since I learned our history five years ago.

There's an expression: *those who cannot remember the past*

are condemned to repeat it. Well, that's bullshit, because we Willows know well our past and look at us now.

The same blocks that have been used for centuries standing in the old library, their surfaces softened by the feet of every other Willow Girl who stood on the same stumps of wood, and all I can think when I see them, the four lined up like they are, is how archaic this is, how fucking unreal. How they can't do this to us.

Yet, here we are.

And they are doing this to us.

But it's not *us*, really.

My shift is marked.

I'm *unclean*.

So it's really my sisters.

Sometimes I'm not sure who I hate more, my own family for allowing this insanity generation after generation, or the Scafoni monsters for demanding the sacrifice.

"It's time," my father says. His voice is grave.

He's aged these last few months. I wonder if that's remorse because it certainly isn't backbone.

I heard he and my mother argue once, exactly once, and then it was over.

He simply accepted it.

Accepted that tonight, his daughters will be made to stand on those horrible blocks while a Scafoni bastard looks us over, prods and pokes us, maybe checks our teeth like you would a horse, before making his choice. Before taking one of my sisters as his for the next three years of her life.

I'm not naive enough to be unsure what that will mean exactly. Maybe my sisters are, but not me.

"Up on the block. Now, Helena."

I look at my sisters who already stand so meekly on their appointed stumps. They're all paler than usual tonight and I swear I can hear their hearts pounding in fear of what's to come.

When I don't move right away, my father painfully takes my arm and lifts me up onto my block and all I can think, the one thing that gives me the slightest hope, is that if Sebastian Scafoni chooses me, I will find some way to end this. I won't condemn my daughters to this fate. My nieces. My granddaughters.

But he won't choose me, and I think that's why my parents are angrier than usual with me.

See, I'm the ugly duckling. At least I'd be considered ugly standing next to my sisters.

And the fact that I'm unclean—not a virgin—means I won't be taken.

The Scafoni bastard will choose one of their precious golden daughters instead.

Golden, to my dark. Golden—quite literally. Sparkling almost, my sisters.

I glance at them as my father attaches the iron shackle to my ankle. He doesn't do this to any of them. They'll do as they're told, even as their gazes bounce from the closed twelve-foot doors to me and back again and again and again.

But I have no protection to offer. Not tonight. Not on this one.

The backs of my eyes burn with tears I refuse to shed.

"How can you do this? How can you allow it?" I ask for the hundredth time. I'm talking to my mother while my father clasps the restraints on my wrists, making sure I won't attack the monsters.

"Better gag her, too."

It's my mother's response to my question and, a moment later, my father does as he's told and ensures my silence.

I hate my mother more, I think. She's a Willow quadruplet. She witnessed a harvesting herself. Witnessed the result of this cruel tradition.

Tradition.

A tradition of kidnapping.

Of breaking.

Of destroying.

I look to my sisters again. Three almost carbon copies of each other, with long blonde hair curling around their shoulders, flowing down their backs, their blue eyes wide with fear.

Well, except in Julia's case.

She's different than the others. She's more…eager. But I don't think she has a clue what they'll do to her.

Me, no one would guess I came from the same batch.

Opposite their gold, my hair is so dark a black, it appears almost blue, with one single, wide streak of silver to relieve the stark shade, a flaw I was born with. And contrasting their cornflower-blue eyes, mine are a midnight sky; there too, the only relief the silver specks that dot them.

They look like my mother. Like perfect dolls.

I look like my great-aunt, also named Helena, down to the silver streak I refuse to dye. She's in her nineties now. I wonder if they had to lock her in her room and steal her wheelchair, so she wouldn't interfere in the ceremony.

Aunt Helena was the chosen girl of her generation. She knows what's in store for us better than anyone.

"They're coming," my mother says.

She has super hearing, I swear, but then, a moment later, I hear them too.

A door slams beyond the library, and the draft blows out a dozen of the thousand candles that light the huge room.

A maid rushes to relight them. No electricity. Tradition, I guess.

If I were Sebastian Scafoni, I'd want to get a good look at the prize I'd be fucking for the next year. And I have no doubt there will be fucking, because what else can break a girl so completely but taking that of all things?

And it's not just the one year. No. We're given for three years. One year for each brother. Oldest to youngest. It used to be four, but now, it's three.

I would pinch my arm to be sure I'm really standing here, that I'm not dreaming, but my hands are bound behind my back, and I can't.

This can't be fucking real. It can't be legal.

And yet here we are, the four of us, naked beneath our translucent, rotting sheaths—I swear I smell the decay on them—standing on our designated blocks, teetering on them. I guess the Willows of the past had smaller feet. And I admit, as I hear their heavy, confident footfalls approaching the ancient wooden doors of the library, I am afraid.

I'm fucking terrified.

Available in all stores!

THANK YOU!

Thanks for reading *Giovanni: a Dark Mafia Romance.* I hope you enjoyed Emilia and Giovanni's story and would consider leaving a review at the store where you purchased this book.

Click here to sign up for my newsletter to receive new release news and updates!

Like my FB Author Page to keep updated on news and giveaways!

I have a FB Fan Group where I share exclusive teasers, giveaways and just fun stuff. Probably TMI :) It's called The Knight Spot. I'd love for you to join us! Just click here!

If you're new to the Benedetti Mafia world, here is the reading order:

Salvatore: a Dark Mafia Romance
Dominic: a Dark Mafia Romance

Sergio: a Dark Mafia Romance (although Sergio's story precedes Salvatore's, it's best to read in this order if you're new to the series. You'll know why when you do.)
Killian: a Dark Mafia Romance
Giovanni: a Dark Mafia Romance

ALSO BY NATASHA KNIGHT

Collateral Damage Duet

Collateral: an Arranged Marriage Mafia Romance

Damage: an Arranged Marriage Mafia Romance

Dark Legacy Trilogy

Taken (Dark Legacy, Book 1)
Torn (Dark Legacy, Book 2)
Twisted (Dark Legacy, Book 3)

MacLeod Brothers

Devil's Bargain

Benedetti Mafia World

Salvatore: a Dark Mafia Romance

Dominic: a Dark Mafia Romance

Sergio: a Dark Mafia Romance

The Benedetti Brothers Box Set (Contains Salvatore, Dominic and Sergio)

Killian: a Dark Mafia Romance

Giovanni: a Dark Mafia Romance

Descent

The Amado Brothers

Dishonorable

Disgraced

Unhinged

Standalone Dark Romance

Deviant

Beautiful Liar

Retribution

Theirs To Take

Captive, Mine

Alpha

Given to the Savage

Taken by the Beast

Claimed by the Beast

Captive's Desire

Protective Custody

Amy's Strict Doctor

Taming Emma

Taming Megan

Taming Naia

Reclaiming Sophie

The Firefighter's Girl

Dangerous Defiance

Her Rogue Knight

Taught To Kneel

Tamed: the Roark Brothers Trilogy

ACKNOWLEDGMENTS

Cover Design by PopKitty Design

Editing by Ann Curtis

Cover Model Domenico Armento

ABOUT THE AUTHOR

USA Today bestselling author of contemporary romance, Natasha Knight specializes in dark, tortured heroes. Happily-Ever-Afters are almost always guaranteed, but she likes to put her characters through hell to get them there. She's evil like that.

www.natasha-knight.com
natasha-knight@outlook.com